Because

of that

Crow

Treasure the Good Memories!

BEVERLEY BRENNA

Red Deer Press

Published in Canada by Red Deer Press, 195 Allstate Parkway, Markham, ON L3R 4T8
Published in the United States by Red Deer Press, 311 Washington Street, Brighton, MA 02135

Library and Archives Canada Cataloguing in Publication
Title: Because of that crow / Beverley Brenna.
Names: Brenna, Beverley, 1962- author.
Identifiers: Canadiana 20200181769 | ISBN 9780889956155 (softcover)
Classification: LCC PS8553.R382 B43 2020 | DDC jC813/.6—dc23

Publisher Cataloging-in-Publication Data (U.S.)
Names: Brenna, Beverley, 1962-, author.
Title: Because of That Crow / Beverley Brenna.
Description: Markham, Ontario : Red Deer Press, 2020.| Summary: "In this moving middle grade
novel, Beverley Brenna expertly demonstrates that sadness isn't something that needs to stay with you,
that positive experiences can repair the tough things that occur in life" -- Provided by publisher.
Identifiers: ISBN 978-0-88995-615-5 (paperback)
Subjects: LCSH Grief—Juvenile fiction. | Loss (Psychology)—Juvenile fiction. | Families -- Juvenile
fiction. | Friendship – Juvenile fiction.| BISAC: JUVENILE FICTION / Social Themes / Death, Grief,
Bereavement. | JUVENILE FICTION / Social Themes / Emotions & Feelings
Classification: LCC PZ7.B746Be |DDC [F] – dc23

Red Deer Press acknowledges with thanks the Canada Council for the Arts
and the Ontario Arts Council for their support of our publishing program.
We acknowledge the financial support of the Government of Canada through the
Canada Book Fund (CBF) for our publishing activities.

ONTARIO ARTS COUNCIL
CONSEIL DES ARTS DE L'ONTARIO
an Ontario government agency
un organisme du gouvernement de l'Ontario

Canada Council   Conseil des arts
for the Arts   du Canada

2 4 6 8 10 9 7 5 3 1

Edited for the Press by Peter Carver
Text and cover design by Tanya Montini
Printed in Canada by Houghton Boston

www.reddeerpress.com

For my sons

CHAPTER ONE

Everything was different because of that crow. Harris knew it. And he was pretty sure the others knew it, too. Grampa, and Mrs. Featherbuster, and Henry and Lucy Harder. And even Tessa. As for Pete—well, Harris figured that old dog probably knew it, too, if truth be told. Pinky was the only one who might not remember anything special about that crow, but she was only three and didn't really understand stuff. Someday she'd find out. When she was older, Harris promised himself he'd tell her everything.

It all started early one morning in April. Harris Albert Olson sat up in bed to find a big black crow tap-tapping its beak against the window right beside his head. One moment, Harris was lying with his face pressed into his familiar Edmonton Oilers patchwork quilt, and the next moment, he was looking straight out at something very surprising. The big crow was huddled against the glass, staring at him out of one beady black eye.

"Quit it!" Harris mumbled. "I'm trying to sleep."

Harris wasn't really trying to sleep. He'd been awake for at least an hour, trying to push away all the things he didn't want to think about, just as he'd been doing since the accident that killed his mom and dad three years ago. Last month had been the anniversary of their death, and Grampa had taken them all out to the cemetery to pay their respects. Tessa placed a few crocuses beside the headstone, and Pinky blew bubbles from the jar of bubble soap that Grampa had brought for her. But Harris kept his fists in his pockets and tried to think about anything except the night they'd died. Because he knew it was his fault. Their dying was all his fault.

Harris jumped out of bed and flapped his arms at the crow, trying to scare it. But the crow kept tapping. And it looked mean, as much as anything could look mean when you only saw one eye. Harris shut the curtain but he could still hear it: tap-tap. Tap-tap-tap. So he opened the curtain and he shoved at the window. He shoved at that old window as hard as he could, but it wouldn't budge. At least, not at first.

The ice had been gone from the prairies for a couple of weeks now and, as far as Harris could see, nothing around the glass was frozen up. He wiggled the handle and pushed again and, with a sudden burst, the window slid wide open and the crow torpedoed out toward the field. But before Harris could close the window, that crow—a big, frowsy hulk of a thing with a pointed black beak and dark, wrinkled feet—that crow flew through the open window and right into Harris's bedroom.

When it landed on his carpet with a solid kind of thud, Harris leaned back and grabbed his quilt. He pulled it right up over his face, and then he pulled it down a bit so he could see. And then he stared, transfixed, at the pointed black beak and the sharp, sharp claws. And he waited for something bad to happen.

What happened wasn't what Harris expected. What happened was that the crow got stuck. Its claws dug into the little braided rug beside the bed and, when it tried to fly, the rug held fast. The bird flapped harder. It flapped furiously. Finally, it raised itself a few inches into the air, but the rug came with it.

Harris laughed. He couldn't help it. The crow looked like one of those stuffed birds in the school library, the ones with glass eyes and their feet glued onto slabs of wood. When Mrs. London, the

7

librarian, moved those stuffed birds around, she'd talk to them. "You won't mind this, Henrietta, my dear," she'd tell the brown partridge before she shoved it to the side to make room for books.

Harris laughed at the crow on his rug and he kept on laughing. The crow turned its head and shot him such an aggrieved glance that Harris grew serious right away. It was clear that this was no laughing matter. At least, no laughing matter to the crow. Its eyes, mean looking through the window, really just looked sad. And its feathers were bedraggled. Even the fluff on the top of its head seemed down on its luck, sticking up in a few stingy clumps, without fully covering what Harris now saw was a bald patch at the back.

After a period of frenzied flapping that got it nowhere, the crow kind of crumpled onto the rug and dropped its head as if it were executing a deep curtsey before a king or queen. Harris waited a moment. Then he slipped out of bed and knelt down. The crow didn't move.

"I'll unhook you," Harris said. "I'll unhook you if you just stay still. And no pecking."

The crow lifted its head and fixed him with a watery stare, but it didn't look angry. Harris stared back. He waited another moment. And then, picking up one wrinkled toe after the other, Harris set the crow free.

As soon as both feet had been disconnected from the rug, the crow straightened up, as if gathering what was left of its dignity, and then it hopped out the door of Harris's bedroom.

"Oh, no!" Harris called. "No, you can't go out there!" But it was too late. The crow was already bouncing along the hallway and then flapping down the stairs. By the time Harris reached the main floor, the crow had perched itself on top of the kitchen cupboards beside Grampa's old china rooster. And there it stayed.

"*Caw*," it said, rather triumphantly. "*Caw-caw!*"

Harris tried everything he could think of. He opened the kitchen door that led onto the deck. He climbed onto a chair and waved his arms. He squirted water from the toy gun Pinky had left by the sink. But nothing ruffled even a single feather on that crow. It sat up on top of the kitchen cupboards and kept its wings tightly folded at its sides. And as much as a bird can look pleased with itself, that crow looked pleased.

Harris ran into the front porch to get the broom, intending to sweep that crow outside once and for all. But it was too late. Grampa was at the foot of the stairs. His thick gray hair was sticking out like porcupine quills and he was eating a handful of chocolate chips.

"Who the heck left the back door open?" Grampa said. "Harris? Tessa? What's going on?" And then Grampa yelled from the kitchen, "And who let this dirty crow in here!"

Then Pinky appeared. One moment she was on the top step, wrapped up tight in her red-and-white quilt, and the next moment she was sliding all the way down. Good thing she had lots of padding. She landed with a heavy thump on the floor in front of Harris, but she didn't cry.

"THAT DIDN'T HURT!" hollered Pinky, throwing off the quilt and clambering to her feet.

Good old Pinky, thought Harris. She never cried, not like the other little kids Harris knew, who seemed to be crying all the time.

Harris could see that Pinky was wearing three of his old T-shirts, the red one on top, with skinny red pajama bottoms sticking out underneath. She looked just like a giant strawberry— big at one end and little at the other.

"How did this dirty crow get inside?" Grampa yelled again.

"I—I don't know," said Harris, bursting into the kitchen. "I was just going to try and get it out."

"You don't know? You don't suppose that when you left the back door open, that crow just flew right in?" Grampa said.

"No. I didn't—" started Harris. But it was no use arguing with Grampa.

Grampa grabbed the broom and started jabbing at the crow. It took off and flapped around the room, and then it headed into the living room with Grampa running after it.

"BIRD!" said Pinky. "BLUEBIRD."

"No, it's black," Harris told her. "It's a crow. A big black crow."

"BLUEBIRD," said Pinky, edging up to the table and pulling her quilt behind her.

"Why is everything so loud down there!" yelled Tessa from the upstairs hallway, slamming herself into the bathroom. "Don't you know some people aren't awake?"

Suddenly the crow came hurtling out of the living room, with Grampa right behind it. This time, it went straight out the open back door and disappeared off the deck. Grampa banged the door shut.

"And stay out!" he yelled. Then he looked at Harris. "You kids are a pile of trouble, you know that?" he grumbled. "A pile of trouble, all the time." But he kind of chuckled as he said it. As if this kind of trouble wasn't so bad.

Pinky tugged on Harris's little finger. She tugged hard and Harris burped, just like always. Then Tessa yelled down from the bathroom, "You're disgusting!" and Harris called back, "No, *you're* disgusting," and the day had begun for everyone in the household. It had begun in earnest.

Grampa slammed around making his Super Deluxe Eggs with bacon. The eggs had cheese and parsley in there—that's what made them so special. Harris's mouth began to water at the sight of them, and he raced upstairs to get dressed. First, however, he peeked into Tessa's room and saw the jewelry box lying on her bed. It was right on top of her quilt. The box was locked, as usual. He wished he knew what was in it. Tessa never let him look, no matter how often he asked. Harris went back into his room, thinking about that. Thinking about what was in Tessa's secret box.

As Harris threw on his clothes, Pinky galloped in to eyeball Chomper. Chomper was a rainbow guppy that had miraculously survived a broken tank, the glass violently cracked during a game of floor hockey a few weeks ago. Now Chomper swam in lazy circles in the smaller tank that Harris was renting from Tessa for twenty-five cents a week. Pinky stared at the fish and then she took a sloppy drink from the mug of water that Harris kept beside his bed.

"Hey, no fair, Pink," Harris laughed. He shook his finger at her, and then he tossed fish food into the tank for Chomper's breakfast. Pinky watched the guppy intently for a few moments, and then she crawled onto the Oilers quilt and pretended to be sleeping. But she kept one eye squinted open, following Harris.

Harris sat down at his desk and looked at the drawing he'd been doing on a big sheet of poster paper. He could hear birds chirping outside. There were robins whistling and chickadees rasping, "*Dee-dee-dee.*" Then a meadowlark added its warbling trill.

In the drawing stood Tessa, with her long blonde hair and her cell phone. She was almost thirteen. Harris was beside her, and he'd made sure to include the freckles on his nose and his spiky red hair sticking up all over. He was three years younger and a fair bit shorter than Tessa. And then there was Pinky, three years old, with pretty much no hair at all, just white-blonde fluff on top and one big curl at the back of her neck that didn't hardly show. She used to have a lot of curls all over her head, but one day she'd locked herself, giggling, in the bathroom with her new plastic scissors, and snip-snap—the curls had come off.

"PINKY!" she said now, tiptoeing over beside his chair and patting the picture.

"Yup, that's you," Harris told her. "Look how bald you are."

"BALD," said Pinky.

"That's what you are because you don't have much hair," he added.

"BALD," said Pinky. "BALD HAIR."

As Harris looked at the drawing, he realized it wasn't nearly finished. Grampa should be in it. But Harris didn't want to draw him without Gramma. They were together in all the photos, and somehow it wouldn't look right putting him in here without her. But Grampa never talked about her, not since she'd died four years ago. Harris didn't feel right about leaving her out, but he also didn't feel right about putting her in. So that left one big empty space.

And the drawing had another big empty space where Mom and Dad should be. But they'd been gone so long that it didn't seem right to include them, either. After all, Pinky—her real name was Ruth— was just a baby when they'd died. Harris had been in Grade 1, and Tessa in Grade 4. The three of them had changed a lot in three years. Harris couldn't imagine his parents beside them now. In fact, he couldn't really imagine his parents at all.

Harris felt a wave of sadness wash over him, and then another. He tried to think about something else, something other than his parents and what had happened that terrible night. But the tide of despair rose up around his chest and, for a moment, he lost his footing and struggled to catch his breath.

Then the meadowlark trilled again, and Harris heard the single pure note of the morning dove that lived over in the woodlot. And then, just as quickly as he'd been swept out into deep water, he was back. Back on solid ground. A bit shaky, but here, nevertheless.

He looked out his bedroom window at the springtime world of stubble fields and pastureland, budding trees, dusty roads, and the nearby marsh from where he could just make out the gabbling of wild geese. No crows, though. He couldn't hear any crows.

Suddenly, just as if someone had opened a window, the memories of the accident came flying back. Because Harris had been in the car with his mom and dad. He had been right there when the drunk driver swerved onto their side of the road and smashed into them.

Harris thought feverishly about that crow. He thought about the dull shine of its feathers, and its wrinkled feet, and the little bald patch on the back of its head. He reached for that crow the way a drowning person might grab onto a rope, and he picked up his pencil again. Maybe he would draw the crow. Maybe he would draw it just as it had looked, standing on the rug in his bedroom.

But then he thought about how the crow would never come back, and he paused, uncertainly. "It'll never come back," he said to himself. "So what's the use?" And then he stood up and slammed his bedroom window. *That crow is gone for good*, he thought. But Harris was wrong. He was definitely wrong about that.

CHAPTER TWO

Pinky took another slurp from the water in Harris's mug and then she grabbed his little finger. Harris gave such an enormous burp that Tessa heard it from the bathroom, even though Grampa had turned on the oven fan and it sounded like an airplane in the house. If Grampa forgot to use the fan when he cooked, the smoke detector would go crazy and then everybody got an earache.

"Harris, you're disgusting!" Tessa yelled.

"You're disgusting!" Harris yelled back. She was probably in there brushing her hair, something she did every morning, prancing around in front of the mirror while nobody else could get into the bathroom. It was a wonder her hair hadn't all fallen out, she brushed it so hard.

Harris had no need of the bathroom mirror. He already knew what he looked like. Big ears. Freckles. Spiky red hair that was sometimes a little longer, sometimes a little shorter, depending on when Grampa had last taken the clippers to it. Right now, it was a little shorter.

"For the love of Pete, get along, you two!" Grampa yelled. "Breakfast's almost ready."

At the sound of his name, Pete started barking from the back deck. Harris jumped down the stairs, two at a time, until he reached the kitchen, where he looked through the glass door at the big brown dog. Pete must have been over in the marsh—his fur was matted and dripping with muddy water, and he looked very happy with himself. Harris sneaked a piece of bacon from the table and threw it outside, where Pete gobbled it so quickly that Harris wondered if he even chewed it at all.

Tessa came thumping down the stairs and flopped into a chair, her phone on her lap. Around her neck was the little key she always carried, hanging on a gold chain. It was the key to that jewelry box. Harris wondered about that box. He wondered what was in it, but he knew Tessa would never tell.

"Jason Beam's texting to ask if I can go with him to the school dance tonight," Tessa said. "His dad could drive us."

"You can't," said Grampa, turning around with a plate of

Super Deluxe Eggs. "You're too young to go to any school dance with any boy." He put the plate in front of Harris.

"I'm almost thirteen!" Tessa yelled.

"I rest my case," said Grampa. He said that a lot. Harris knew that Grampa used to be a lawyer. But when his house had burned down, taking Gramma with it, Grampa had moved in with them. That was before the car accident. Then, after the car accident, Grampa had quit his job because, he said, nobody in their right mind could have more than one full-time job. "And my full-time job is you three kids," he told them often enough. "My job is you three, like it or not."

Harris threw another piece of bacon out to Pete, who was standing with his legs apart and licking his lips in anticipation. Then Harris flung himself at his plate and piled bacon on top of the eggs. As he chewed, he hummed that song, the song that Xavier, a kid at school, sang every morning when he collected the registers.

Harris hummed the tune in between bites and thought of the words Xavier always sang. *Oh, when the Saints ... go marching in ... Oh, when the Saints go marching in ....* He wondered what that song was about. Where would Saints be marching?

"Twenty minutes until the bus gets here!" Grampa said. "Make sure you've got everything you need because I don't want to be driving to school in an hour." Grampa seemed grumpier than usual, but that's how it went. Sometimes he was less grumpy and sometimes he was more grumpy.

"Jason's texting me about tonight!" said Tessa. "The dance! He says his mom and dad could both drive us!"

"You're not going to that dance with Jason Beam!" Grampa said. "But I'll drive you there like I promised and pick you up at eleven, and you can dance with anybody you like."

"That sucks!" yelled Tessa. "Maybe I won't even go!"

Even Tessa was crankier than usual today. Maybe Grampa's grumpiness was contagious. Harris looked carefully at his sister. Her hair was longer than it used to be. And her nose looked longer, too. And there was a frown line between her eyes. Harris wondered if it was permanent.

Grampa lifted Pinky from one of the big chairs and into her highchair. Then he set down a plate of bacon and eggs, all chopped up, along with Pinky's little gold spoon.

"A RIDDLE!" begged Pinky. "GIMME A RIDDLE!"

"What animal says 'Caw-caw,'" said Harris.

"BLUEBIRD!" Pinky hollered.

"No," Harris said. "A crow! It was a crow, Pinky." She giggled.

"Maybe I won't even go to that stupid dance!" repeated Tessa.

"Fine," said Grampa calmly. "No skin off my back."

"Do you want everyone to think I'm a geek?" cried Tessa.

"It's Friday," Grampa said. "They'll have forgotten all about the dance by Monday."

Friday. It was Friday! Harris felt his stomach lurch. He shoveled in another forkful of eggs. Today he was supposed to hand in his poster for the Grade 4 Science Fair. Mrs. Featherbuster was expecting it. She'd already given him a week's extension. And she wasn't a teacher you wanted to mess with. Even if her name was Featherbuster, which you'd think would give her a sense of humor.

"No excuses, Harris Olson," she'd said firmly, peering at him over her glasses. "On my desk by nine o'clock Friday morning! *Or Else!*"

Harris gulped down his last bite of eggs, but his mouth was so dry that his tongue stuck to the back of his throat. Just like it did in hockey when he played goal and his team was losing.

Maybe I can work on the poster during the bus ride, Harris thought.

"Dear God, please let me finish my science poster while I'm on the school bus," he whispered. Except he'd already used up all the poster paper. Maybe he could just plan the poster now and finish it at school.

"Dear God, please let me finish my science poster on time," muttered Harris. God sure hadn't helped him much lately. He'd had detention last week for what he'd said to Marsha Abbot, and then Grampa'd gotten a school letter about that broken window, even though it had been an accident. But somehow saying the prayer made him feel a little better.

"The Science Fair is the most important part of our Grade 4 year," Mrs. Featherbuster had said the first week of school. "It will be our Crowning Glory. We are aiming to win the Grade 4 Living Science Award for our school division. And I know we can do it! We can do it this year for sure and vindicate ourselves!"

Harris didn't know what *vindicate* meant, but when the teacher looked at them over her glasses, Harris knew she meant business. And she was talking in her big voice, the voice she kept for Warnings and Other Important Messages.

He knew all about what had happened last year. His best friend was in that class. Not only did last year's Grade 4s lose the contest, a class from Dundurn School had won—and their teacher was Mrs. Featherbuster's ex-boyfriend!

"How can she have a boyfriend when she's married?" Harris had asked.

"She got divorced and then she got this boyfriend and he left her just before the Science Fair. And then his class won," Grenade had said. "And she was so mad, she gave us extra work for the whole rest of the year."

"You each need an original poster that answers an important question," Mrs. Featherbuster had told them more than once. "Your project has to be something that no one else has ever done. Something you won't find on the Internet. Ask a good question and pursue the answer. Be curious! Discover! Make our school proud!"

Every month she'd been mentioning the Science Fair. And now it was April. And everybody in class had submitted a poster, except for Harris.

"The bus is at the next farm," said Grampa, leaning toward the kitchen window. "Time to hustle."

Harris pushed himself away from the table and grabbed his backpack from the corner. Then he stuffed a piece of paper and a pen into the side pouch. *Or Else.* That's what she'd said. *By nine o'clock Friday morning. Or Else.* So, he'd better think of an idea. And fast!

But instead of heading out to the bus, Harris tore up the stairs, and then tiptoed into Grampa's bedroom and slid open his sock drawer. There was the bag of chocolate chips. He poured out a giant handful and stuffed them into his mouth, hoping they'd make him feel better. But they just made his mouth dry again. And then he suddenly felt really jumpy. He took a look at the old poster of water lilies over Grampa's dresser, but even that didn't calm him down. When he left the bedroom, he saw Grampa's fiddle leaning into the wall behind the door. It wasn't in its case or anything, just leaning there all dusty. Seeing it there gave Harris a funny, empty feeling inside.

"Lunch," Grampa said, throwing him the bag as Harris ran past after Tessa who was already halfway down the long driveway. "And after school, we'll pick up those lambs from the Harders," Grampa called.

Three lambs. There were going to be three orphan lambs this

year. The Olson kids would bottle-feed them and care for them until they could be returned to their flock. Just like they had done last year, and the year before. But even the thought of the lambs couldn't interest Harris now. He had to think of that science project!

As he ran down the driveway, Harris thought about school. The last kid that got an *Or Else* was Carlyle Sunday, and he'd had to write a ten-page essay about *Rocks and Minerals*. That was the topic of the science unit they'd just started. *Rocks and Minerals*. And Carlyle Sunday had to read his essay aloud in class. Harris imagined himself standing up in front of everyone, in front of the whole class, in front of Jessica Shewchuk, with her big green eyes on him, reading out loud. *Rocks and Minerals*. It would be horrible. It would be terrible and horrible.

Gravel from the driveway flew in all directions as he kicked his feet, and he saw that his breath was making dragon smoke in the chilly air. He puffed toward Tessa, sending dragon smoke her way.

"Stop it," she said. "I'm texting."

Harris kicked harder at the gravel, and then a flash of dark wings made him turn and look up. A crow was flying overhead toward the woodlot where Harris could see other crows roosting in the bare poplars. As Harris watched, a couple of the bigger birds darted forward, flapping and pecking at the newcomer, who immediately swerved back toward Harris and Tessa.

As the school bus lurched to a halt beside them, the crow flew past again and perched on top of a fencepost.

"It's you!" cried Harris. "You're back!"

The crow watched as they climbed onto the bus, and then it seemed to be staring in at Mrs. Jessup, the bus driver. When the bus moved forward, the crow flew alongside, looking through the window at Harris.

When the bus reached top speed, Harris lost sight of the bird. But he had the feeling that it was up there, flying just above the bus, watching over. Harris had the feeling that crow was watching over him, but he didn't know why.

He was still thinking about the crow when the school bus pulled into the yards of the other houses around the ring of acreages, and then the bigger farms along the range road. One after the other, kids climbed onto the bus. Some of the younger ones carried blankets. One even had a pillow.

Harris was still thinking about the crow when the bus stopped to collect the remaining high school kids that lived along the township road close to the school. And he was still thinking about the crow when the bus pulled into the school parking lot and rolled to a halt beside the front door of Clavet Composite School.

CHAPTER THREE

As Harris climbed out of his seat, he remembered that science project. Or rather, his lack of a science project. *Or Else.* Maybe the punishment wouldn't be an essay about *Rocks and Minerals* this time, since Carlyle Sunday had already done that. Maybe she'd assign him an essay about something different. *Lakes and Rivers of Saskatchewan.* Harris shuddered. Horrible. That would be horrible and terrible.

He'd have to stand there, in front of the whole class, reading aloud about *Lakes and Rivers.* He'd look up and Jessica Shewchuk would be looking at him with her big green eyes, and he would have to say, "*Lakes and Rivers ...*" He couldn't stand it. He knew he wouldn't be able to stand it. He moved down the aisle toward the door of the bus.

"Don't forget your jacket, Harris!" yelled Jennifer Onion. She lived beside them on the next acreage and she was always bossing

Harris from the back of the bus. Just because she was in Grade 9 didn't mean she knew everything.

"I wasn't going to forget it," Harris said, leaning back to grab the jacket.

"You did yesterday!" Jennifer Onion was the kind of person who always had to have the last word. "Mrs. Jessup had to bring it into the school."

Harris jumped off the bus behind Tessa. She used to sit with him sometimes on the bus, and she'd even talk to him. And play games. But not now. Not anymore. Jason Beam was waiting on the pavement for her and Tessa ran up to him as if her life depended on it.

"Do you think he'll change his mind?" Jason Beam asked.

"No way. The grumpy old fart," Harris heard Tessa say.

Grampa? They must be talking about Grampa, Harris thought. He wondered why Grampa got so cranky. Harris remembered games of badminton behind his grandparents' house in the city—and cards, while Gramma poured lemonade and set out bowls of that toffee popcorn Grampa used to eat all the time. Grampa wasn't grumpy then. He'd tell all sorts of stories about old times and play music on his fiddle. And Mom and Dad would dance, and Gramma would sing "Yellow Submarine."

As Harris walked around the side of the school to the junior boot room, he suddenly remembered the crow and took a long look around. There was no sign of it. Probably it was really gone now. Gone for good. He pulled open the big door and went inside. The glass was still taped over from where his soccer ball had cracked it during playoffs. He'd been practicing with rebounds against the school and somehow missed the brick wall completely. And smashed the glass.

Next year he'd be able to use the Grade 5 entrance, but this year he was still stuck here in this wing with the younger kids. Some of the guys his age were already inside, changing their shoes and waiting for the bell. Harris felt a ray of hope as he asked if anyone wanted to help with his science project. But the others just acted superior. Mike Morin said, "If you'd done it on time, you wouldn't be worrying about it now."

"No kidding!" Harris told him.

Then Marsha Abbott said, "You're gonna be in big trouble." Harris remembered last week when he'd called her Marsha Rabbit because of her teeth. It was what everybody used to call her before her mom came and talked to the class. He was sorry as soon as he'd said it, but he couldn't take it back. And then he got a detention and missed the very last recess soccer game.

"Hey, Grenade!" Harris called as his best friend came into the boot room. Grenade always sneaked back from the senior wing for a visit whenever he could. And his name was really Renae. But when Harris met him years ago, he'd heard *Grenade* instead of *Renae* and the name had stuck.

"Am I glad to see you!" Harris said. "How was Track?"

Harris had wanted to join Track, too, but Grampa had said no—they needed a sports break between hockey season and baseball season.

"Good," said Grenade. "Lots of running. How's Chomper?"

"Good," Harris said. "Good as a fish can be, I guess."

Grenade pulled a loonie out of his pocket.

"Here's some money for that tank," he said. "It'll pay your rent to Tessa for ..." he calculated, "... about a month."

"You don't have to pay," said Harris.

"Nah, take it," said Grenade. "I broke your old tank, didn't I? Anyways, I'm loaded. My grandparents came last weekend and gave me a whole jar of coins." So Harris put the money into his pocket.

"I'm trying to finish my science project," Harris said.

"What's it about?" asked Grenade.

"Well, I don't have a topic yet," said Harris. "But as soon as I get a topic, I'm going to finish my poster."

"You're out of luck, man," said Grenade. "You can't do a project that quick. Last year, I drew what the sky looks like at night. My question was, *What stars are over us right now?* And it took me a long time to get it right."

"Well, I can't do anything somebody's already done," said Harris, feeling cross.

"Anyways, we didn't win anything last year," said Grenade. "Mrs. F. was mad."

"I know," said Harris.

"And Mrs F.'s ex-boyfriend won last year," Grenade went on. "She was really mad about that."

"I know!" Harris repeated. "Anyways, I need to think of something fast!"

"Why not cover your eyes all weekend and then see if things look any better," said Grenade.

"That's dumb," Harris said.

"How about coming to live at my house and then seeing if anybody notices you're gone?" said Grenade.

"That's so dumb," Harris said.

"You're on your own," said Grenade when the bell rang. "Good luck!" He started to walk away, but then he turned back.

"I remember a kid last year who didn't have a poster," he said. "Mrs F. made him say a speech."

Harris's mouth went very dry.

"Yeah, I remember it really clearly," Grenade continued. "We all laughed at him. It was about *Saskatchewan Fish*."

"*Saskatchewan Fish!*" Harris whispered, his legs weak. Then he saw Jessica Shewchuk walking ahead down the hallway, with her hair all bunched up at the back as if she'd slept on it wrong. Harris slowed down. He didn't want Jessica Shewchuk to see him like this.

As he hung his backpack on the peg at the back of the classroom, his hands were still shaking. He sat down at his desk and looked at the board. That's where Mrs. Featherbuster kept the Bell Work. When they came into the classroom, they were supposed to get a pencil and write the Bell Work assignment into their Bell Work notebook. Then they had five minutes to finish it before the teacher started the school day.

Friday, April 6, Harris wrote. Then he copied the assignment.

Make a list of as many types of rocks as you can think of.

"Rocks," he muttered. "Boring!"

He wrote down the title: *Types of Rocks.* Under it, he wrote: *Fossils.* But then he started to worry. Were fossils rocks or were fossils just the spaces other things made in rocks? He erased *Fossils.*

Mrs. Featherbuster came into the classroom and went over to her desk. She was wearing a big flowery dress. She looked around the room and rubbed her eyes. Something about her always looked sorrowful, thought Harris—even today, even when she was wearing that bright dress. She smiled at the class, a big, warm smile, but there was sorrow underneath. Harris could feel it.

Harris put his head down and tried to think of other types of rocks. Maybe his teacher had forgotten about the science fair. Or forgotten that his work was due today.

He wrote "Rock Band." Then he erased it. When he lifted his head, Mrs. Featherbuster was walking toward him.

"Gravel," he wrote, over the erase marks. "Stones. Mountains. Boulders." He looked up and she was standing at the front of his aisle.

"Potash," he wrote feverishly. He knew potash was a rock

34

and that you could find it around here. That's why there were a lot of potash mines in Saskatchewan.

Then he got another idea. "Diamond." He knew that was a rock because he remembered his mom saying once, "Don't worry about getting me a bigger rock. I like the one I have now."

His mother had been talking about her wedding ring. It had a tiny diamond in it. He remembered they were all watching television, and some commercial came on, and that's when she said it. They were all watching television, and they were eating chips and drinking something Mom called Ambrosia that you made by mixing fruit punch and ginger ale. The commercial was about diamond rings. And Mom looked at Dad and said, "Don't you worry about getting me a bigger rock. I like the one I have now."

Harris felt the tide rising again inside of him, and by the time he saw Mrs. Featherbuster beside his desk, like a big bouquet of flowers, he could hardly breathe.

"So, what about that science project?" she said.

"What? Yeah. I ... I'm working on it," he muttered.

"Well," she said. "You and I can talk about it at recess." She turned on her heel and went toward the front of the room.

Recess? Harris thought. *I'll have to miss recess?* He looked at his Bell Work and started to erase. He erased everything except *Potash and Diamond,* and then he erased those, too.

Mike Morin poked him in the back.

"You shoulda finished it last week," he said.

"Quit it," Harris muttered.

Mike Morin poked him again.

"If you'd finished it last week, you wouldn't hafta miss recess and the start of football," he said.

And then Harris turned around and hit Mike Morin in the nose. He didn't plan to do it. He just did it.

CHAPTER FOUR

In an instant, Mrs. Featherbuster was standing beside Harris with her hands on his shoulders.

"You stop that! No fighting!" she said.

Mike Morin had blood coming out of his nose. Not much blood, just a little trickle that he smeared onto his chin.

"Mike, are you okay?" the teacher asked. When he nodded, she told him to go and get a wet paper towel. Then she said, "Harris, come out into the hallway with me."

When Mrs. Featherbuster got into the hallway, she eased herself down on one of the little chairs she kept out there. Then she pulled a chair over for Harris. She looked like a whole garden, all in bloom.

"Why did you do that?" she said. She was frowning hard.

"I don't know," Harris said.

He really didn't know why he'd done it. Mike Morin bugged

him all the time. But he bugged Mike Morin, too. This was no different.

"What's going on?" said Mrs. Featherbuster.

"No," said Harris. "No, he ... I ..." And suddenly a sob burst out of him, and then another. He pressed his face into the wall. Probably everybody in the hallway could hear him. Probably everybody in the whole school could hear him. But he couldn't stop crying.

"Sit out here until you calm down," Mrs. Featherbuster said. "And then I'll be back."

It was like he was under water, gulping for air and struggling for shore. For a few minutes, he didn't think he was going to get there. But he did. He took a deep shuddering breath and wiped his eyes.

Then Mrs. Featherbuster was back with Mike Morin.

"You two boys have something to talk about," she said and pulled up a chair for Mike. She had on her big voice this time, the voice that she used for Warnings and Other Important Messages.

Harris looked at Mike Morin. Mike Morin looked at Harris.

"Sorry," said Mike Morin, even though his nose was still bleeding a little and he hadn't done any of the hitting.

"Sorry," said Harris.

"Okay, then," sighed Mrs. Featherbuster. She gave them each a measuring look. "As long as you've both learned something, you can come back into the classroom."

Learned something? thought Harris. He looked at Mike Morin. Mike Morin looked at him. Then Mike Morin nodded. So Harris nodded. And then he followed Mike Morin inside.

As Harris sat down at his desk, he started wondering about those chocolate chips. They'd gotten him so jumpy. Probably he shouldn't eat them before school. Maybe he shouldn't eat them at all. But Grampa ate them. That's why he kept a bag in that drawer. Because the ones in the kitchen cupboard were always gone. And Grampa needed them to keep from smoking.

Harris suddenly remembered that his mom had eaten lots of chocolate chips, too. She'd kept hers in the fridge. She hadn't been trying to quit smoking, though. She'd just liked them.

"Race you outside at recess," Mike Morin whispered.

"Okay," Harris whispered back. But then he remembered he wasn't going outside at recess.

Harris saw that everybody had already put their Bell Work away and that now it was Silent Reading. The classroom was so quiet that he could hear Marsha Abbott's stomach growl from one row over. He thought about offering her a carrot, but then he remembered they couldn't tease her anymore. The more he thought about not teasing her, the more he wanted to tease her.

Mrs. Featherbuster was sitting at her desk with her head on one hand and looking up at the ceiling. *She's staring up there as if the sky is falling,* thought Harris. *And she's thinking of something really sad.* Then she looked directly at Harris and her expression changed. She held up a book.

Harris knew what that meant. He didn't have a book in his desk, so he went over to the classroom library and looked around. Then he picked up a graphic novel and skimmed the back cover. That's what they were supposed to do to see if the book interested them. *Skim and Scan.* Harris wasn't sure of the difference, so he just *Skimmed.*

The book was about a car accident. Harris put it down like a hot potato.

Suddenly he felt awful. His head hurt, his stomach hurt, and, worst of all, he thought he was going to start crying again! He started to back out of the reading corner.

"Is okay?" Bana Manafort was standing beside him. "Is okay?" she asked. She'd only been in Canada a few months and already she was speaking English pretty well. But Harris couldn't answer.

Instead, he grabbed a bathroom pass from the wall and raced into the hallway where he tripped over one of the little chairs the teacher had left there. He got up quickly, rubbed his knee, and took a drink of water at the fountain. "Okay," he said to himself. "Everything's gonna be okay."

Except everything wasn't okay. Ever since they'd gone to the graveside, it was like Harris was reliving the accident over and over. He saw the car lights coming right toward them and then he felt the impact. Felt their car rearing up and then flipping over into the slough. He was hanging by his seat belt with the strap digging into his shoulder and water was coming in. He struggled out of the seatbelt, and he could see the big white airbag that had filled up the front seats. His dad pressed the button to unlock the doors and yelled, "Get out! Harris, get out of here!"

Harris took another drink from the fountain and, around him, the school hallway came back into focus. Then he heard someone coming. It was Xavier. And Xavier was singing, as usual.

It was Xavier's job to collect the register from every teacher. He took them to the school secretary, Mr. Bayer, who recorded all the information about who was away. Once it had been Tessa's turn to be Xavier's helper. Today it was Molly Stringer's turn. She was one of Tessa's Arch Enemies. They used to be friends, but Molly had been hanging around with Jason Beam earlier in the year and now she hated Tessa more than anything. At least, that's what Tessa said.

When Xavier passed Harris, he reached out and patted him on the head.

"Good kid," he said, his brown eyes shining. And then he kept on singing.

Xavier was the kind of person who needed to do the same thing at the same time each day because it made him feel comfortable. Xavier had something different about his brain. Harris couldn't remember the name of it. Every day Xavier collected the registers and sang about the Saints, and then he went back into his classroom and did his work. At the end of the day, he brought the registers back to the teachers, but then he sang something else. At the end of the day, Xavier sang, "Swing Low, Sweet Chariot." He sang it at the end of every day.

Now, Xavier's big, rich voice filled the hallway and Harris took a deep breath and listened.

> *Oh, when the Saints*
> *Go marching in*
> *Oh, when the Saints go marching in*

How I want to be in that number

When the Saints go marching in.

Harris suddenly knew what that song was about. It was about dying. It was about the Saints marching into heaven, and how the singer wanted to go there with them.

He knew his parents were in heaven. That's what the minister had said at the funeral, and other people had told him the same thing. But were his parents angels? He didn't know. He didn't really know much about angels.

Suddenly his classroom door opened and Mrs. Featherbuster poked her head into the hallway.

"Here you are again," she said. "Harris?"

He shook his head.

"No," he said. "I was just ... I was just thirsty." He turned around and took another drink at the fountain.

"Well, come on back inside because we're changing our shoes for gym," she said.

So many things were bouncing around in his head that he reached up both hands to push them away. His anger at Mike Morin. All the crying. Thinking about heaven. And angels. He stumbled back into the classroom.

When Harris pulled on his gym shoes, he felt them pinch. They were too small. His shoes were already too small, even though he'd just gotten them in January.

And as Harris stood there with his feet squeezed into those too-tight shoes, he thought about dying. He thought about dying and this is what he thought: that everybody was going to die sometime or other. And go to heaven. That didn't bother him. The idea of dying didn't bother him. It was living that was hard sometimes. That's what Harris thought as he walked down the hallway with his class, his toes pinching harder and harder with every step. Sometimes living was the hardest thing.

On their way to the gym, the class walked past Xavier collecting registers in the primary end. He was singing:

Oh, when the stars fall from the sky

Oh, when the stars fall from the sky ...

Harris waved at him and Xavier reached out and patted Harris on the head. Then he patted everybody else on the head, at least everybody he could reach before they went into the gymnasium. A couple of the girls were too tall for him, but he got most of the boys.

Harris wanted to ask Xavier something, but Molly Stringer was standing there with him, and Harris didn't want to ask anything in front of Molly Stringer. What he wanted to ask was: "How come you like these two songs, Xavier?" But Molly Stringer was standing there, and she had some kind of sparkly stuff in her eyebrows, and Harris couldn't talk with her around.

So, Harris didn't ask Xavier those questions. Or anything. He just walked into the gym and crossed his fingers that it was going to be Dodgeball.

Please, God, let it be Dodgeball, he thought to himself.

CHAPTER FIVE

It wasn't Dodgeball. It was a new game called Double Ball. Mrs. Featherbuster told them that in Cree it was called *Pitisowewepahikan*. They used a special stick to move two balls connected by a leather string, and there was lots of running. So much running that Harris's feet throbbed hard inside the too-tight shoes.

When Mrs. Featherbuster ran, her orange runners were like big butterflies flapping around her flowered dress. Soon Harris forgot about his feet. He passed the balls to Bana Manafort and she passed to him. She had great aim.

"Good!" he yelled at her. "Good!"

The game was so fast and fun that Harris liked it just as much as Dodgeball. He liked it so much that he forgot he was supposed to stay in for recess. After gym, Mrs. Featherbuster had to come out into the hall and call him back into the classroom with her voice for Warnings and Other Important Messages. Everybody in the hallway heard. Probably everybody in the whole school heard.

On his way back into the classroom, Harris brushed past Mike Morin. Mike Morin didn't say anything, and Harris didn't punch him in the nose. *I guess we have an Understanding,* Harris thought.

That's what Grampa called it when Harris was fighting with Tessa and they stopped fighting. *Having an Understanding.* Harris wished all the people fighting in wars right now would get one. If everyone had an *Understanding,* it would be peaceful everywhere. *If God can do anything at all,* Harris thought, *he should deal with Understandings before anything else.*

After Harris had flopped down at his desk, Bana Manafort came up to him. "Is okay?" she whispered. "Okay?"

"Yeah," he said. "Thanks."

Mrs. Featherbuster eased herself down onto the desk across the aisle. "You haven't got a poster, have you?" she said.

"No," said Harris. "But I have an idea. An idea that I'm working on."

He looked hard at the flowers on her skirt.

47

"So ... what's your idea?" Mrs. Featherbuster asked.

Harris thought. He thought hard. He thought about Xavier, and why he sang those songs, and he thought about Molly Stringer, and how her eyebrows got so sparkly. His mind was skimming over all sorts of things that didn't have anything to do with science projects. How grouchy his Grampa was, and how Tessa never sat with him anymore on the school bus. And how Mike Morin's nose had looked with the trickle of blood coming out of it. Then a sudden movement at the window made him jump. There, outside, on the window ledge, tapping its beak against the glass, was the crow!

"My crow!" he said.

"Your ... your crow!" repeated Mrs. Featherbuster. "Do you have ... is that your ... a crow?"

"Yup," said Harris. "He's ... he's mine, all right."

"Oh. Well ... okay," the teacher said. "So, your project is about crows?" Mrs. Featherbuster darted another look at the crow, who was still tap-tapping against the glass. "It looks ... does it want to come in?"

"I think so," said Harris. "It came inside our house this morning, until Grampa ran it outside."

The crow was now using its wrinkled black feet to try and pry at the glass.

"I don't think ... we shouldn't really let it in," said Mrs. Featherbuster. "Although it does seem ... it seems very persistent!"

"*Caw,*" said the crow from outside the window. "*Caw-caw!*"

Mrs. Featherbuster went over to the glass to have a closer look.

"It seems ... glad to see us," she said after a moment. "And as if it really wants to tell us something."

Harris nodded.

"*Caw, caw-caw,*" rasped the crow.

"How did you ... did you catch it? And tame it?" asked the teacher.

"Well, it ... it kind of found me," said Harris.

"And how long have you ... how long have you had it?" she asked kind of dreamily. Her gaze was fixed on that crow. It seemed as if she couldn't take her eyes off it.

"Well ..." started Harris.

"It looks ... it looks like an old, old man," Mrs. Featherbuster said softly.

Harris was afraid to say he'd only had the crow for three hours, because maybe she would think that wasn't long enough for a science project, so he blurted, "A week. I mean a month. I've had it a month."

"A month," she repeated.

"So, this is a good topic, right?" Harris asked. When she looked at him blankly, he added, "For my poster?"

"Well, yes," she said. "Yes, I should think so. There are all sorts of things I don't know about crows, and I will look forward to hearing about them."

Harris brightened.

"But you absolutely have to have everything finished by Monday," she said firmly. "We will have everything ready for the judges and it will be our big chance to win."

Harris nodded. Maybe there'd still be time to get outside for recess if he hurried.

"I'll give you a note to take home so that your grandfather will help," she added, still looking at the crow. "Do you know ..." she went on, more to herself than to Harris, "... do you know what this crow makes me think of?"

Harris shook his head. He hoped she'd hurry up and finish talking so he could go outside.

"When I was a little girl, there was an old man who lived at the end of our street. I've forgotten his name. I've forgotten his name, it was so long ago. I'd even forgotten him, if you want to know the truth. I'd forgotten him until this very moment. But this crow ... this crow reminds me of him, in a very strange way. I could almost think that he and this crow had something ... something very much in common."

Harris shifted uncomfortably on his chair. He really wanted to get outside.

"Sometimes ... sometimes in the summer," the teacher went on in a dreamy voice, "when this fellow was out on his porch in the evenings, we used to go over there. All the neighborhood kids. We used to go over there and he would kind of light up when he saw us. He would invite us to sit down, and then he'd tell us stories."

"Stories," said Harris, trying to speed her up.

"Stories about adventures he'd had. Working as a trapeze artist in a circus. Exploring the Amazon. He made his fortune in the Gold Rush, or so he said. I was just a little kid then, when I listened to those stories. It was the only time in my life I had no cares. No cares at all. I'd never really been sick. Certainly, I'd not had cancer—that came a lot later. No husband who left me with four kids to raise. No sick mother whose meals I have to take over every night and who is not grateful for any of them."

Harris swallowed. It was almost as if she was hypnotized. Did Mrs. Featherbuster really mean to be telling him about this personal stuff?

"I listened to those stories," she went on, "and dreamed about how wonderful my own life would be. Oh," she laughed sadly, "I had no cares at all in those days." Then she stared hard at Harris as if suddenly remembering he was there. "And no letters to write over the noon hour, to send home with my students about their late work," she added sternly. "Remember, you need everything finished by Monday. *Or Else.*"

"Okay," Harris said quickly.

"And do you need to take home a sheet of poster paper? Or do you have one?" asked the teacher.

"I need one," said Harris.

"What's the name of this crow?" Mrs. Featherbuster asked.

"Pardon?" asked Harris.

"You said this was your crow. What's its name?"

Harris looked at his teacher. Then he looked at the crow. The name "Featherbuster" occurred to him, but he knew better than to say it. He swallowed hard, so "Featherbuster" wouldn't pop out by mistake, and then he took a deep breath and looked through the window at the crow. It was peering in at them with one beady eye, and pecking at the glass with its sharp beak. Relief washed over him that his earlier lie about having a project hadn't been discovered. And it wasn't a lie, not really. He did have a project. At least, he did now.

Suddenly a word jumped into his head. *Vindicate.* But that wasn't a name. That wasn't really a name.

"*Vinny,*" said Harris. "I call it *Vinny.*"

"*Vinny,*" Mrs. Featherbuster murmured. "Exactly! That's exactly right!"

"Can I go out for recess now?" asked Harris.

"Recess? Well, certainly. Yes, you may," the teacher said softly, still looking out at that crow.

"Vinny," she repeated, touching one finger to the glass. "*Mr. Vinny.* Yes. Yes, that's what his name was."

CHAPTER SIX

Harris tore down the hallway and into the boot room. But he didn't get farther than that. He didn't get farther than that because the bell rang and he knew it was no use. Now he wouldn't get outside at all. He wondered how his team had done. They'd only just started touch football and he hoped they'd won today's game.

"Did you think of your science project?" called Jessica Shewchuk. She was the first one into the school, as usual. It was almost as if she liked school, she got in there so fast.

"Yeah, well, it's going to be about my crow," Harris told her.

"Your crow!" she said. Her eyes looked greener than ever. Harris knew that if he stared into those eyes too long, he'd be unable to say anything.

"They kill all the baby robins," she told him. "Fitfully and in starts, my mother says."

"No," Harris said quickly. "No, I don't think they do," and he made a mental note to look that up on the Internet. One thing he was certain of—Vinny wouldn't kill baby robins. Not unless they attacked first, or something.

"And other songbirds. If it wasn't for crows, we'd have a lot more songbirds around here," Jessica Shewchuk went on.

"No," said Harris again, but weakly. Those green eyes. It was all he could do to force out that single word.

"Anyways, my project is on the environment," said Jessica Shewchuk. "I gave everybody at church a survey to see how much their family recycles. Then I compared that to the national average. My question was, *How does our United Church community compare to the national average in terms of recycling?* I'll probably win the prize for Best Project," she said. "Even though I had to make up the national average because I couldn't find out exactly what it was."

"Oh," said Harris, looking down at his feet.

"What question are you asking?" she said.

"What question?" said Harris.

"What question about crows. Like, what exactly is your poster going to tell us about them?"

"Uh. Well. Everything," said Harris as other kids pushed

past them. "Well, not everything. Just some things. Just some things about crows." He felt as if all the words that were in him might pour out, right now, in the warmth of Jessica Shewchuk's green gaze. "The most important things," he added. "The most important things about crows, I mean."

"Well, okay. Bye," she said, and galloped off into their classroom. Her hair had kind of flattened since Harris had seen it before school. Now it was only a little lopsided.

"We lost," said Mike Morin dejectedly, heading into the classroom, too.

"Dang it," said Harris.

The rest of the day passed in a kind of blur. Harris kept an eye on the window but, no matter how hard he looked, he didn't see Vinny again.

In last period, Mrs. London asked the whole class to line up, and then she led them to the library. Harris walked between Mike Morin and Bana Manafort. Mrs. London read them all a chapter from a book by Farley Mowat, a book called *Owls in the Family*. It took place a long time ago on the prairie near here, and because it was about owls, she'd brought the stuffed owl over to listen. *Winston Churchill* was its name.

"If you don't mind," she'd said to the class, "I'll just bring Winston Churchill over here to listen to this part. I think Winston Churchill will be mightily interested because this book has some true facts about owls, even though it's fiction. We might even label it *narrative non-fiction*."

Harris almost laughed aloud at the fierce look in Winston Churchill's eyes as Mrs. London read. Harris didn't mind Mrs. London. She smelled kind of fruity.

"Do you have any other books like this?" he asked her at the end of the period. "Do you have any other books like this, except about crows?"

"About crows," said Mrs. London. "Well, I'll have to have a look. If I find something, I'll let you know. I don't really remember any stories about crows."

"Or narrative non-fiction," said Harris. "That would be okay, too. Or other kinds of non-fiction. Or anything, basically. About crows."

"Crows," said Bana Manafort. "Crows in my homeland. Lots of crows. Gray. Gray but black hood on the head."

"Crows eat all the baby robins, that's what I know about crows," said Jessica Shewchuk, who was hovering nearby.

"No!" said Harris. "They don't!" But he didn't look at her when he said it.

As the class left the library, Harris heard Xavier in the hallway singing his end-of-the-day song:

> *Swing low, sweet chariot,*
>
> *Comin' for to carry me home.*
>
> *Swing low, sweet chariot,*
>
> *Comin' for to carry me home.*

The song stuck with Harris long after Xavier had finished collecting the registers. Harris thought about the words and wondered again why Xavier liked them so much. He thought so hard that the song seemed to carve itself into his head, and then, even when he tried to stop thinking about it, the words came back anyways:

> *I looked over Jordan, and what did I see?*
>
> *Comin' for to carry me home.*
>
> *A band of angels comin' after me,*
>
> *Comin' for to carry me home.*

"A band of angels comin' after me. Comin' for to carry me home," he repeated to himself, liking the sound of the words and the picture they conjured in his mind. He could just see those angels flying him home. Maybe they could be his parents. Offering him a lift.

Or maybe *home* meant something else. Maybe it meant *heaven*. Maybe this song was really about dying.

Harris wanted to run over to the senior wing and talk to Xavier. He wanted to ask, "How come you like only two songs? And how come they're both about dying?" He wanted to run over there right now and ask Xavier these questions. But he didn't.

When it was time to get onto the school bus, Jennifer Onion was there on the sidewalk ahead of him.

"Don't leave your jacket at school," she said. "Or your lunch kit."

"I'm not," said Harris crossly, and then he ran back inside to get them. Why did Jennifer Onion have to be so bossy, and why was she always right?

"Oh, Harris, I'm glad I caught you!" said Mrs. London, charging down the hallway toward him. "I found these three books. One is about crows, but it's a little on the easy side. The other two are about birds in general, but they both have information in them about crows. I've signed all three books out under your name. I hope you can use them!"

"Thanks," said Harris, taking the books. "Thanks, Mrs. London!"

"And I took the liberty," she panted, "of reading a little bit about crows myself. Because—because I was wondering about that saying, you know, where one person tells another to *go eat crow* ..."

Harris shook his head. He hadn't heard that saying before.

"You know, where two people are arguing," Mrs. London went on, "and when one wins the argument, she might say to the other, *You can go eat crow!*"

Harris shook his head again.

"Well, I found out about it. From the Internet. As the story goes, in the War of 1812, a British officer made an American soldier eat part of a crow the American had shot in British territory. So, when someone is forced to admit a mistake, that's when we say, *Go eat crow*."

"Gross," Harris said. "Eating crow."

"It's mostly dark meat," said Mrs. London, smiling. "At least, that's what it says on the Internet."

"Thanks," said Harris. "Thanks a lot." He tucked the books into his knapsack and ran for the bus. As soon as he got outside the school, he looked around, but he didn't see Vinny.

Maybe the crow was gone for good this time. Maybe that crow was really gone for good. Harris crossed his fingers.

"Please, God, if you can help me out here, please let me finish my science poster. By Monday," he whispered. Then he swallowed and added, "And please let Vinny come back."

Harris knew that this prayer wasn't as important as his other prayer about all the countries in the world coming to an *Understanding*, but he trusted that God would put the two prayers in the right order.

"And please make our science projects so good that Mrs. Featherbuster can be vindicated," he said, "in front of her ex-boyfriend." He was glad he'd used the word vindicated. He hoped a word like that would help God treat his request seriously.

Tessa was still standing out on the pavement beside Jason Beam when the bus driver slammed shut the door and called, "Everybody on?"

"No! My sister's still outside," Harris called.

Mrs. Jessup opened the door and yelled, "We're leaving, Tessa! Are you on or off?"

Tessa said one more thing to Jason Beam, and then she ran over to the bus and climbed the stairs.

"Someone's got a boyfriend," said the bus driver, and a few kids laughed, but Harris didn't. Tessa wasn't laughing, so he knew she didn't think it was very funny. Instead of sitting with her friends, she flopped down in the empty seat beside him.

"How come you're sitting alone today?" she asked.

"Grenade's got Track practice. Before and after school," Harris said.

"Oh. So ... how was your day?" she asked.

"Okay," said Harris, surprised that she was even talking to him.

"Heard you told your teacher that you've got a pet crow," she said as the bus pulled out of the parking lot and onto the grid road.

"Well, maybe I do," said Harris. "Maybe I do."

"Maybe you do, but maybe you don't," said Tessa. "And you shouldn't say you do if you don't."

Just at that moment, Harris saw it, flying along beside the bus. *Vinny!*

"Look!" he said to Tessa. "Look!"

As they watched, the crow swooped down and peered at them through the window. Harris could see the downy tufts on top of its head parting in the wind, and the long feathers on its wings rippling as it accelerated. Then the crow lifted up and out of sight.

"Wow, would you look at that," Tessa said. "Maybe it *is* your pet." She craned her neck toward the window to look out. "I can't see it anymore. Can you?"

"Nope," said Harris. "But it'll be back. I think it'll be back. It kind of comes and goes whenever it wants."

"It reminds me of something," said Tessa softly.

"An old man?" asked Harris. That was what it had looked like to Mrs. Featherbuster.

"No, not an old man," said Tessa. "A baby. A brand-new baby, all bright-eyed and curious about the world. And happy. Really happy."

"Like Pinky?" asked Harris. "Does it remind you of Pinky?"

"A little bit," Tessa mused. "And you. It's a lot like you when you were a baby."

"I don't remember," said Harris. "I don't remember any of that."

"Well, I do," said Tessa. "I remember all of it." She closed her lips tight and her face kind of froze. Then her right hand reached for the little key that hung around her neck and she pinched it between her fingers.

"Tessa, do you think Mom and Dad are angels?" Harris blurted, looking hard away from his sister and out the window where the crow's black shape was still imprinted on his mind. "Angels in God's heaven?"

"Maybe," she said after a moment. "Yeah, maybe."

"Do you think they're watching over us?" Harris asked.

"Sometimes," she answered in a small, tight voice. "And sometimes not."

Harris thought about that. Did she mean that sometimes they were watching and sometimes they weren't? Or did she mean that she wasn't really sure whether Mom and Dad watched over them at all? He stole a quick look at her and decided not to ask. At least, not right now. The whole of her looked frozen now.

After a few minutes, Tessa let go of the little key and looked at Harris. "You know, Grampa named you."

"He did?" Harris asked, surprised.

"Yeah. When Mom and Dad brought you home from the hospital, they still hadn't decided on a name. Mom wanted to call you Chandler, after some guy she saw on TV. Dad wanted to call you Storm Davis, after somebody in sports. And Grampa and Gramma came over, and finally Grampa said, 'It's time to name that kid, already. Call him Harris Albert.' So they did."

"Harris Albert Olson," said Harris, the way a hockey

announcer might say it. He'd always liked his name and imagined it coming from the TV when he was a pro-hockey player.

"After Grampa," said Tessa.

"What?" asked Harris. "No. Grampa's name is Al."

"Harris Albert," Tessa said. "Look at his driver's license sometime. Harris Albert Stead. Mom was Maggie Stead before she changed her name to Olson when she married Dad."

"How come I didn't know this?" Harris asked, but Tessa didn't answer. She merely tucked that little key on its chain back under her T-shirt.

"Tessa, do you remember any other stuff?" Harris asked. "Like ... other stuff about me?" But Tessa was looking out the window again as if searching for that crow, and Harris couldn't tell if she was looking for the crow to help herself remember, or if she was looking for the crow to help herself forget. Either way, it was like the lid of a box had slammed shut with all Tessa's memories locked tight inside.

CHAPTER SEVEN

After school, Tessa grabbed a cookie from the table and went up to her bedroom and slammed the door. Then Pinky stomped into the kitchen and climbed onto a chair between the table and the kitchen counter. She tipped it back until it touched the kitchen counter, and then banged it down toward the table.

"Stop rocking that chair or you're gonna get hurt," said Grampa. But Pinky did it again.

Harris handed Grampa the letter from Mrs. Featherbuster and then took a cookie from the plate. It was kind of plain looking, that cookie. He took a bite. And then another. There weren't any chocolate chips in it, not even one.

"Bang!" went Pinky's chair a third time.

When Grampa had finished reading the letter from Harris's teacher, he frowned.

"Harris, you're getting into a lot of trouble at school!" he said.

"No," said Harris. "Well, just one thing. With Mike Morin. But didn't Mrs. Featherbuster write to you about my science project?"

"That, too," said Grampa. "You're over a week late and the final poster is due on Monday."

"Well, yeah," said Harris.

"And last week there was a broken window, and then making fun of that girl's rabbit teeth."

"We're not supposed to call them *rabbit teeth*," said Harris, flushing. "I know. I get it."

Pinky slammed down on the big chair again and Grampa looked at her.

"No more of that!" he said. "You're gonna get hurt!"

Then Grampa looked back at Harris.

"Your teacher wants me to stress to you the seriousness of fighting," said Grampa. "You know that fighting is serious, right?"

"Well, neither of us was laughing," said Harris.

"This letter will stay with all the other ones in your school folder," said Grampa. "That folder is getting kind of full."

Harris didn't answer. Pinky grabbed a cookie from the plate and started breaking it into little pieces.

"Is the fight over?" asked Grampa.

"Yeah," said Harris.

"Nothing wrong with fighting," Grampa said. "As long as you both know you're fighting, and you also know when it's over. And it better be over now."

"Yeah," said Harris again. "It's over."

"Because if it isn't, we'll invite that boy and his parents to come and talk to us."

Pinky started breaking a second cookie overtop the first.

"No, we're good," Harris said. "Me and him are good."

Grampa gave Harris a stern look.

"Make sure you are good," he said. "Or we'll need to talk again."

"Okay, okay," said Harris. Grampa didn't need to go on about things. Anyways, it really wasn't his business. It really wasn't his business what Harris did. Or didn't do. He was just an old Grampa who didn't know much about anything except being grouchy.

"And now about that science project," Grampa said.

"For Pete's sake, I can do it myself," said Harris. Pete started barking from the deck, but Harris ignored him.

"It's going to be about that crow, if you have to know all about it. I told my teacher. And she's fine with it. Now all I have to do is make the poster!"

"So, you don't need my help?" asked Grampa. "Because it needs to be at school on Monday morning!"

"I know! I'll get it done!" said Harris.

Slam went Pinky's chair, and this time she fell hard onto the tabletop.

"Pinky!" said Grampa. "I told you to stop doing that!"

She slid down off the table with her face turned the other way, and then she walked into the living room. But she didn't cry.

Harris took another cookie and then ran upstairs, where he unrolled the poster paper on his floor. He took out the three bird books and put them on top, to flatten it out a little.

"Ready to go and get those lambs?" called Grampa. "Henry Harder's waiting for us."

"Yeah, I'm coming," said Harris, looking down at the blank poster paper. If he could just get a title, he'd be almost finished. That was how it was with projects. Once you had a title, you were nearly done. But he couldn't think of a title, other than just "Crows" and he was pretty sure his teacher wanted something more than that.

CHAPTER EIGHT

When Grampa stopped the truck in the Harders' farmyard, animals came flying out from all directions. Four cats. A bunch of chickens. A goat. At first, Pete raced from one side of the truck to the other, poking his nose over the tailgate and lolling out his tongue. But when three dogs headed for the truck, tails wagging, Pete lay down flat inside the truck box, whimpered once, and then played dead, just like he always did when he met other dogs.

Harris patted the dogs so Pete would know there was nothing to worry about, but it had little effect on him. They bounded over to Grampa, who opened the tailgate and then pulled out some dog biscuits from his shirt pocket.

"See, Pete! Nothing to worry about!" called Harris, as Grampa gave a biscuit to each of the Harders' dogs. But Pete didn't move. When his eyes were shut like that, Harris knew that Pete thought nobody could see him.

"Okay, stay there, you big chicken," Harris told him. "You're going to miss all the fun."

Pete twitched his left ear and kept his eyes closed.

The goat was nosing something in the straw at the edge of the garden and Harris went over to investigate. A miniature pig wriggled out of the straw and the goat bunted it. Then the pig grunted and started to run.

"Stop that!" Harris told the goat. It turned around and rolled its eyes. Then it ran after the pig and bunted it again. Fitfully and in starts.

"How would you like someone to bunt you?" Harris yelled.

"Never mind that goat!" called Henry Harder, backing out of the house, the screen door banging behind him. He was carrying a kitchen chair. And he was wearing a bright red shirt. With his white hair and beard, he looked more like Santa Claus than ever. But sad. Still sad. *He'd be one of the most unhappiest Santa Clauses ever,* Harris thought. Sadness hung on Henry Harder the way his clothes hung on him. In folds and wrinkles.

"That pig needs the exercise," Henry Harder said, putting the chair down in a shady spot under a big old apple tree whose leaves were just starting to burst out. "She'd stay in the straw all day long if we let her." He went back into the house for a minute. Then he came out with his wife. He was holding her hand and leading her along as if she were a child. As if she were Pinky, thought Harris, Pinky who was home right now, with Tessa babysitting.

After Henry Harder had settled Lucy in the chair and put a blanket on her lap, he came over and shook hands with Grampa.

"Good to see you, Al," Henry said.

"How are you, Henry?" Grampa said. Then he looked over at Lucy. "Howdy, Lucy," he called.

Lucy looked at him but didn't answer. There was no expression on her face. Harris thought he'd never seen anyone look so much like an empty sheet of paper than Lucy Harder at that moment.

"She's a bit lost today," Henry Harder said. "It's been like this for a couple of weeks, now. I'm ... I guess we're losing her," he added, his voice breaking. "She doesn't know who I am most days. But at least she's not fussing about anything."

Grampa and Henry Harder walked ahead to the pasture and, for a while, Harris could hear them talking.

"About raising teenage girls," Grampa was saying. "When your daughters were that age ..."

"Well, times are different now, that's for sure," Henry Harder answered. "It's a different generation."

"Our kids always had to be home before midnight," Grampa went on.

Every now and then, Henry turned back to check on Lucy. Harris knew that Lucy had an illness in her mind that made her forget things. When Harris first knew her, she'd always ask him to choose between a cookie and a doughnut. He usually picked the doughnut because it was bigger. But she'd stopped asking. Probably because of that illness.

The three dogs bumped up against Grampa's legs, and Harris followed behind to keep an eye on the goat. It had lost interest in the pig, but now it was jumping up at the clothesline. Someone had thrown clothes over the line and the goat was licking at them with its long pink tongue.

Harris wondered how clean something was after a goat has licked it. *Can you catch diseases from goat spit?* Too bad he couldn't use that question for his science project. But it would be too difficult to measure, and somebody—maybe him—could get sick testing it out.

Henry Harder went into the pasture and started putting the

lambs into new-looking cardboard crates. Harris glanced at the big ewes nearby, wondering if some of them were the mothers of these lambs, or if their mothers were dead.

The adult sheep all had little narrow eyes and big yellow teeth. Their heads looked like bricks. Big fuzzy bricks. And the babies looked just like their parents, only smaller and without the teeth. The three lambs that Henry Harder was crating were so skinny you could count their ribs, and their legs were like sticks.

Harris took a good look at the lamb in the crate closest to him. It looked like a bag of skin with its bones rolling around inside. Its eyes were red and its wool was patchy with mottled pink skin showing through. And it smelled. Boy, did it smell!

"You're going to get fat," he told it. "You're going to get nice and fat and then we'll bring you back here."

He wondered how come these lambs needed help. Maybe one of the ewes had twins and couldn't feed them both. Or maybe a ewe took a dislike to its lamb, for no reason. Or maybe the mothers had all died giving birth. Grampa had talked to him and Tessa other times about all these possibilities, but Mr. Harder never said exactly what kind of circumstances each lamb came from. *These lambs could be orphans, just like me*, Harris thought suddenly. His heart thumped heavily as he watched Henry Harder putting lids on the crates. They had holes in them so air could get in.

Henry Harder gave a crate to Grampa and one to Harris. Then he took the third crate and they carried the lambs back to the truck. The crate was surprisingly light in Harris's arms. Suddenly, Harris was startled by a pair of black wings that swooped down near his head, and he almost dropped his lamb.

"Vinny!" he called, and the crow wheeled around and touched down on top of his crate.

"Harris!" warned Grampa. "Get that filthy crow away!"

Before Harris could respond, Lucy called out, "Hello, you all," and then Vinny took off again.

"Lucy!" said Henry Harder, turning as his wife approached them. His voice was pure gladness. "You're back!"

"I guess I am," she said, walking over to the little group. "I was watching that bird and it—it reminded me of something. It really did."

"An old man?" Harris blurted. "Or a baby?"

"No, no ..." said Lucy, smiling. "When it flew overhead, I kind of rose up to meet it. And then I just felt like my old self again."

She smiled at Harris. "Would you like a cookie or a doughnut?" she asked.

Henry had put his box down right there in a patch of mud, and now he wrapped his arms around his wife. On his face was something Harris took a minute to name. *Joy,* he thought finally. *It's joy.*

"I'm so happy you're here," Henry Harder told Lucy, and his voice was husky. "It's been a long time, Honey."

"Oh, now Henry, everything is fine. I'll just get this boy something nice," she said. "Except ... I'm not sure what I have ..." She began to look a bit worried.

"It's okay," Harris told her quickly. "I don't need anything. Anyways, we'd better get these lambs home."

"Well, next time, I'll just have to give you a doughnut and a cookie," she said kindly, waving him on.

Grampa slid his crate into the back of the truck box beside Pete, and Harris did the same. Then Grampa went back for the crate Henry Harder had been carrying, carefully walking past Henry and Lucy. They were still standing together on the grass, leaning toward each other. The goat was back, running in circles around them. The three dogs had disappeared.

When Grampa got to the truck and stood there a moment, it looked to Harris as if his grandfather was rubbing away tears, but Harris couldn't be sure. It had started to rain, and maybe it was just rain on Grampa's cheeks. Maybe all those wet spots were only rain.

CHAPTER NINE

After Grampa shoved the last crate over the tailgate of the truck beside the others, Pete's eyebrows twitched, but nothing else on him moved. Grampa took out a handkerchief and rubbed at his ruddy face.

"Big chicken," said Harris to Pete. "You're missing all the fun."

Grampa's face was red and kind of puffy. Harris tried to think of something else to say.

"Can Pete have a biscuit?" he asked, finally.

Grampa cleared his throat and took another dog biscuit out of his pocket. Harris put the dog biscuit a few inches away from Pete's nose, and, without opening his eyes, Pete squinched forward until he could reach the biscuit with his lips. Then he ate it.

"Good boy!" said Harris.

Pete licked his lips. Then he opened one eye and, when he didn't see those other dogs around anymore, he jumped up and took a quick sniff at the crates. Then he gazed expectantly at Harris, as if hoping for another treat.

"That dog of yours is a terrible scaredy-cat," said Grampa.

"He's always been afraid of stuff," said Harris. "Strangers. Other dogs. Birds, especially magpies. Thunderstorms. Everything except food. He's not afraid of food."

"That's for sure," snorted Grampa, stomping around to the driver's side. Harris climbed into the front seat beside him. When Grampa gunned the engine, three things happened. First, the goat ran straight for the truck and jumped right onto their hood. Second, Pete hit the deck, closed his eyes and played dead. And third, the rain started coming down in buckets.

"Tarnation!" said Grampa, honking the horn. The goat rolled its eyes and then tumbled off into the wet grass, surprisingly landing on its feet and then running off into the pasture. Harris wished they could have a goat or two. But he knew it was no use asking.

He glanced into the back of the truck and Pete was still lying down, the rain making little rivers on his rusty brown coat.

"And goats," said Harris. "Pete's also afraid of goats!"

Grampa turned the truck around and headed down the

driveway and then onto the main road. Harris looked into the back of the truck box. There were the three crates, just where they'd left them. The water was making little pools on top and running down through the holes. That wouldn't bother the lambs, though. They were used to getting wet.

Pete didn't seem bothered by the rain, either. He was standing up, his fur all matted and soggy, and he was looking out of the truck box, his tongue lolling out. And suddenly, as Harris watched, a dark shape dove down toward the truck and landed on the dog's head. It was Vinny. And while that was surprising enough, it wasn't the most surprising thing. The most surprising thing was that Pete didn't seem to mind. He didn't mind the crow sitting up there, surfing along, its feathers ruffling in the wind.

"Hey!" Harris cried.

Grampa looked into the rear-view mirror.

"Well, would you look at that!" he said. "Tarnation!"

"I'm calling that crow *Vinny*," said Harris. "And it's going to be in my science project. And I sure hope we can keep it." Harris looked back at the crow again. It was still surfing on top of Pete's head.

"Can we keep it?" asked Harris.

"Never heard of a crow for a pet," muttered Grampa.

"Vinny could be a special case," said Harris. "Anyways, there was this guy that had pet baby owls. This guy in a book. His name was Farley Mowat. Mrs. London's reading us a story about him and it's a true story. Actually, it's ... it's narrative non-fiction. About him and those owls. And if owls can be pets, then so can crows!"

"Narrative non-fiction," mumbled Grampa. "What will they think of next?"

"But could I keep it?" Harris asked again.

"Wild things belong in the wild," Grampa said.

"I don't think the wild wants this crow," Harris said. "It flew over to the crows in the woodlot this morning, but they chased it away. They were mean, pecking at it and everything! So ... I rest my case," he said.

"Hmmph," said Grampa, and Harris knew he'd just have to wait for the answer. He'd just have to wait and see.

Harris thought about that crow. He thought about it as hard as he could. Vinny really was a special case. Harris wondered how Vinny knew enough to recognize him every time. That crow sure had a good memory. Maybe he'd put that on his poster. Stuff about crows and their good memories.

The rain pelted down and the ditches near the road were close to overflowing. It suddenly looked very much like the place where the accident had happened, a little over three years ago. It had happened when they were driving home from Harris's last hockey game of the season. Grampa was home looking after baby Ruth and Tessa was over at a friend's.

Harris knew that his hockey game hadn't caused the accident. He'd talked about that with a grief counselor after the funeral. About the drunk driver, and about all the other factors, including weather, that had contributed to the crash. But somehow this year, he'd begun to think about things again. To think about things and his role in them. Learning about the concept of personal responsibility in Health class made him wonder about what he'd done during the emergency. What he'd done and not done.

As Harris remembered that night, he began to feel sick. He looked around to try and distract himself. But the windshield wipers were pounding back and forth, back and forth, and the truck was too hot, and he couldn't see anything but rain.

"I never had to do much in science," Grampa was saying. "We just had to memorize things and then write tests."

"I wish we had that," Harris managed to say.

"And if we worked hard in school, we never had homework," Grampa told him. "Until law school. You don't know what work is until you go to law school. That's where I started smoking." Grampa stopped and shook his head and then he muttered, "Darn fool thing to do."

Grampa had been a lawyer. Harris already knew that. There were cases that came forward, and you had to argue them. A case was like a story. A story about something.

Before he'd moved in with them, Grampa used to be good at telling all sorts of stories, especially at bedtime. Harris remembered one about a magic lamp and a genie that came out and gave you wishes. And he remembered another about a lion with a thorn in its paw, and the man who pulled the thorn out and became the lion's friend. Harris didn't think those stories were true. Once Grampa had told him about how his own grandfather had cleaned his false teeth in the bucket that pulled their water from the well, and how Grampa had tried not to drink out of the bucket for a long time afterwards. That story, Harris knew, was a true one.

"Work," repeated Grampa. He had a kind of pinched look on his face.

Harris suddenly wanted to ask about Gramma, but the words he wanted to say got stuck in his throat. How had the fire started? He really wanted to know about that.

Harris shifted in his seat. Suddenly he felt even sicker and he thought he was going to throw up.

And then he did throw up.

And what happened after that was that Grampa gagged and pulled the truck to the side of the road and then went for a little walk. While he was walking, the rain stopped. And then between the two of them, they got Harris cleaned up and tossed his dirty jeans into the back of the truck. Pete ran over to the other side of the truck box and Vinny circled at a distance.

After using an old rag to mop up the floor of the truck, the job was done. Done as good as could be expected. Then they just started driving again, but they kept the windows open. Harris sat shivering in his underwear.

"You're okay now, right?" Grampa asked every few minutes.

Harris nodded.

"You're not going to throw up again?" Grampa asked. "Because you should tell me if you are. Tell me first, not afterwards."

"No," said Harris. "No. It was just ... I ... this road reminded

84

me of something. All the water. It was just like ..." he stopped and looked over at Grampa, who was clutching the steering wheel as if he was hanging on for dear life.

Grampa's face looked as if he had a pain somewhere. A really bad pain. Harris stopped talking and Grampa didn't talk any more, either. Harris swallowed the words he wanted to say, the words about how it felt when the car had flipped over, and the water had come in, and his dad had told him to get out. *Get out of here,* he'd said as the car started to sink deeper. And how, once Harris was out of the car and swimming through the dark water, he knew he should have gone back there. He could see the car disappearing into the slough. He should have gone back there to help, to help them somehow, but he hadn't. He just hadn't. The water was too deep, and it was all he could do to swim to the edge. His body was numb with cold and he couldn't feel his arms and legs. But he should have gone back. He just should have.

And all the while Harris was thinking these things, and not saying them, Grampa was just looking straight ahead and driving. And when they got home, Grampa said, "Go clean up and get on warm clothes. Then you and Tessa can get the milk ready for those lambs while I make supper." And Harris knew that the time to say what he needed to say had passed.

Pete jumped down from the truck box with Harris's dirty jeans in his mouth. Then he streaked around the yard for a while so that nobody, not even Grampa, could catch him. Tessa and Pinky stood giggling on the deck, shouting encouragement, but Harris couldn't tell who they were rooting for. Finally, Grampa caught one pant leg in his hand, and pulled and pulled, and after a short tug-of-war, Grampa went triumphantly into the house with Harris's pants while Pete slunk off to his doghouse.

Tessa said, "Harris, how come Pete had your pants in the first place?"

And then Harris said, "Never mind!"

And then Grampa said, "Hurry up, now, and let's get these lambs fed."

Henry Harder had put a bag of powdered milk into one of the lamb crates. After Harris found some dry pants and washed his hands and face, he got out the old pop bottles and nipples from last year and made up three bottles.

While Grampa barbecued, Tessa, Pinky, and Harris tried to get the lambs to drink. They carried them into the garage, because it was raining again, but they left the lambs in their soggy crates, because their damp, dirty wool smelled so bad. Pete lay down with his head on his paws, watching, but the crow was nowhere in sight. Every now and then Pete twitched his eyebrows, and Harris wondered what he was thinking.

Pinky's lamb seemed to know what to do right from the start. It grabbed the nipple in its lips and sucked and sucked from the bottle until all the milk was gone. Pinky laughed.

"BALD!" she said, pointing at the lamb. "BALD HAIR!"

"No, Pinky," Harris told her. "You are bald. Kind of bald, anyways. And the lamb has wool."

"BALD WOOL," she said, and laughed again.

"Couldn't you have picked ones that don't smell awful?" said Tessa, wrinkling up her nose as she poked the bottle at her lamb. "Phew!"

"You'd smell bad, too, if you lay around in a field of poop," Harris told her.

"You're disgusting," she said.

"You're disgusting!" Harris yelled back.

"For the love of Pete!" called Grampa. "Stop fighting! The steaks are ready—Al's Famous Steaks! Come and get 'em!"

Pete started barking like crazy, and Tessa carried her lamb and Pinky's lamb, one at a time, to the shed in the back pasture. But Harris's lamb hadn't had any of the milk yet. And it could barely lift its head, let alone drink. Harris tried pushing the bottle into its mouth from various angles, but nothing worked. Finally, he picked up the lamb, like they used to do with Pinky, and cradled it on its back. Then he gave it the bottle like you'd feed a baby. It didn't really suck, but it watched him the whole time with its beady red eyes, and swallowed when the milk spilled down its throat.

"I think it's working!" Harris said. And suddenly he was singing. He was singing ever so softly. *"Oh, when the Saints. Go marching in! Oh, when the Saints. Go. Marching in."*

He was singing Xavier's song, as much of it as he could remember, and by the time he'd finished, the milk was all gone and the lamb's eyes were shut. Harris carried it gently over to the shed and put it beside the others in the straw. Then he latched the door and followed Tessa and Pinky toward the house.

There was a flash of lightning and then a big boom of thunder. Pete streaked in front of Harris and squeezed himself through the doorway, bolting upstairs before anyone could stop him.

"Just leave him," said Grampa, setting a big dish of salad on the table. "He'll be hiding in my shower again, and we can just leave him there until the storm's passed."

Grampa leaned down with a cloth to wash Pinky's hands. She squirmed away and grabbed one of the big chairs.

"No, Ruth," said Grampa. "You need to sit in your highchair. After I wash your hands."

The big chair fell over with a bang.

"See, you're too little for that," said Grampa. "Come and we'll wash your hands in the sink."

"You stink!" said Tessa to Harris.

"Do not! You stink!" Harris yelled, but Grampa agreed with Tessa.

"Go change your clothes and wash up," he said. "And then you can eat. And then we'll all drive Tessa to the dance."

"STINK PINK!" yelled Pinky as Grampa buckled her into her highchair. "STINK PINK!"

"I'm not going to the dance unless I can stay 'til the end," said Tessa. "And it ends at midnight!"

"I'll be there at eleven," said Grampa firmly. "And that's final.

CHAPTER TEN

Pinky and Harris had to go along for the ride when Grampa drove Tessa to the dance. They had to go because there wasn't anyone at home to watch Pinky, and Harris wasn't old enough to babysit her himself. Rain was still falling and the air was chilly. Harris watched the windshield wipers go back and forth, back and forth, and he felt sleepy by the time they reached the school.

When they pulled into the parking lot, Harris saw Jason Beam standing on the sidewalk. He was talking with Molly Stringer. Tessa must have seen him, too.

"Oh, that's just great!" Tessa hissed. "Let me out right here!"

"You're welcome," said Grampa, opening his door. "I'm just going into the school for a minute, Harris. I'll be right back. Watch Pinky, okay?"

"Okay," said Harris. He looked at her and thought of Humpty Dumpty.

"Rest your head here on the back of the front seat," he told Pinky, unbuckling her seat belt. "And then I'll teach you a new rhyme." He started to chant "Humpty Dumpty" and Pinky giggled.

In no time, Grampa was back.

"See, I can babysit her just fine," Harris said, hauling Pinky into her car seat. "Why can't I stay home with her alone next time?"

"Not until you're twelve," said Grampa, starting the engine.

When they got back home, Harris unbuckled Pinky's seat belt again and she jumped out of her car seat. Then she stretched her chin over the front seat of the truck and looked at Grampa and bellowed, "HUMPTY DUMPTY SAT ON A WALL!"

"Humpty Dumpty ..." Harris continued.

"HAD A GREAT FALL!" she screamed.

Grampa burst into unexpected laughter. It was good to see Grampa laugh. Harris laughed along with him. Even Pinky chortled, proud of herself.

"EGG," she said, patting herself on the head. "BALD EGG."

"Good girl," Harris told her.

"GOOD EGG!" she squealed.

"Time to feed the lambs again," said Grampa. He swung Pinky out of the truck and gave her a big kiss on the cheek.

"Already?" Harris grumbled. "They ate before supper!"

"Their stomachs are small, remember?" Grampa said. "Five feedings a day. It's good for you all to have some responsibility for something other than yourselves. Service is a good teacher."

The word *responsibility* bounced around in Harris's head and he kicked at clumps of dirt along the front flowerbed.

"Are you okay, son?" asked Grampa, holding the door for him. "Is everything okay?"

"Yeah," said Harris, pushing past on his way to the kitchen. "Yeah, I guess."

The rain had stopped. Harris and Pinky walked through the cold damp air to the shed after Harris had fixed the bottles of milk. The lambs still smelled bad, and Harris laughed at the way Pinky wrinkled her nose at them. They sat down and fed the first two lambs, while the third one just lay quietly in the straw. It wasn't even watching them.

The bigger two lambs seemed to know exactly what the bottle was for. Once they started to suck, the milk disappeared quickly. But the third lamb, the smallest one, didn't seem to remember anything. It had to be held again before it would drink. Harris had to cradle it like a baby so the milk would run down its throat. Pinky sat beside Harris, wrinkling her nose and watching him feed the lamb.

"STINK," she said.

"You stink," Harris told her.

She giggled. "NO. YOU!"

"Stink Pink!" Harris sang, and she giggled harder.

"STINK PINK, STINK PINK!" she repeated, standing up and jumping around so hard that one of her rubber boots came off and her sock got all muddy. At least, Harris hoped it was just mud.

When the third bottle was empty, Grampa appeared with a heat lamp.

"Not more dirty clothes!" he said. Harris looked at Pinky, and then he realized that his jeans were muddy, too.

Grampa hung the heat lamp on the inside wall of the shed and lifted the lambs under it where it was nice and warm. The lambs couldn't stay out in the pasture because of predators. Coyotes and even eagles could take a young lamb. And, anyways, it was too cold tonight to be out in the open.

"I think I'll call this one *Violet*," Harris said, looking down at the smallest lamb.

"You might not want to name it just yet," Grampa said, lifting

Pinky up onto his hip. "It doesn't look as if it's doing too well. Best not to name it yet."

"*Violet*," Harris whispered to the lamb, just the same, before he closed the shed door.

While Grampa put Pinky to bed, Harris kicked around the house for a few minutes.

"Can I play on the Internet until bedtime?" he called.

"Sure," Grampa called back. "But only games on those sites we've bookmarked."

Harris scrolled through a bunch of online games, but he really didn't feel like playing anything. Next he googled "crows." A website popped up that had a lot of information about them, and one thing it said was:

> *Contrary to popular belief, crows will not remove all the songbirds from an area. They do eat other young birds, but without the crows, many of these birds wouldn't live anyway. So having crows present, or not, doesn't make a difference to the songbird population.*

"There," said Harris, thinking about Jessica Shewchuk.

"I told you! So, you can just go and ... go and ... eat crow!" He laughed to himself. That would teach her. Except ... except Harris didn't really want to teach Jessica Shewchuk anything. Not when she had green eyes like that, looking at him the way she did.

Harris picked up the three books and flipped through them. The picture book didn't say very much about crows, but it said a few things. The other two books were filled with more information about all sorts of birds, but each had a small section on crows, and Harris read through everything.

When Harris was finished with the books, he grabbed the picture he'd been drawing that morning, the one of himself, Pinky, and Tessa. It didn't feel finished. There was way too much empty space and Harris didn't know how to fill it. He slid the picture behind his desk where he couldn't see it anymore. Then he laid out the new sheet of poster paper and printed across the top in big letters, "All About Crows."

Underneath that, he printed, "Crows live here on the prairies and all over North America. Different kinds of crows live almost every place in the world. They eat grain, earthworms, and snakes."

Underneath that, he wrote, "Crows may eat baby robins, but only if they need to be eaten."

Next, he printed, "Crows are one of the most intelligent kinds of birds and they have a very good memory."

And then he added, "Crows can remember lots of things, like how to get inside a house or a school."

Harris thought for a minute after writing down this last part. He thought for a minute, and what he was thinking was: How could Vinny know how to get into a house or a school, unless that crow had been inside before?

Harris looked back at his poster. He couldn't be wasting time now. He just had to get finished. He had to get finished his work.

He had a lot of space left on the poster and he couldn't think of anything else to add, so he drew a picture of Vinny down in the bottom corner. But there was still more space to fill. He got a black felt marker and traced over everything he'd put on the poster so far.

Then Harris put the marker down and listened. He listened to the rumbling of the furnace, and he listened to the wind pushing against the window. Then he heard Grampa across the hall, reading a story to Pinky. He didn't hear Tessa, because she was still at that dance. Tessa wouldn't be home for a long time yet. Harris stood up and thought for a moment. Then he tiptoed into Tessa's room and looked at that jewelry box. It was sitting on her dresser. He picked it up and tried to lift the lid. But it was locked, as usual.

Harris sat down on Tessa's quilt and wondered what was in that old jewelry box. What could Tessa be keeping in there that was so special? *Maybe I could break it open,* he thought. But he didn't. He just shoved it back where he'd found it.

Then Harris crept into Grampa's bedroom and opened the sock drawer. Chocolate chips were spilling out of the bag. Maybe that was his fault from this morning. Harris quickly ate all the stray ones, staring at Grampa's old poster of water lilies. He liked how the colors in the picture were all blurred together. *Pencil crayons wouldn't do that. But maybe pastels would.* Harris took another big handful of the chocolate chips. And then he carefully closed the bag.

By the time he got back to his own room, Harris was feeling bouncy. So he jumped on his bed until Grampa yelled, "No more jumping!"

"Aw, Grampa, just a few more minutes!"

"No. And did you brush your teeth?"

"Yeah," said Harris, crossing his fingers.

"You did not," Grampa said. "Get in there and brush."

Harris went and looked for the toothpaste.

"We don't have any more of the good toothpaste," he yelled.

"Never mind ... just use what's there," Grampa called back.

It was mint. Harris hated mint. It always made his mouth burn. But he put a little on his toothbrush. When he was done, he bounded into his room and looked out his window, bouncing harder. Everything looked blurry when he did that. Like Grampa's poster of water lilies.

Those water lilies were made by somebody named *Monet*, Harris remembered. Over a hundred years ago. *Maybe they're made with pastels,* Harris thought.

In the warm glow of the yard light, Harris could see the back deck from his bedroom window. Pete was outside again, standing by his food bowl, and that crow was beside him. It was picking up pieces of kibble and laying them out. Then, one at a time, it was dipping them in water. And eating them.

"Okay, into bed," said Grampa, coming into the room. "In a few minutes, I've got to go and get Tessa. Jennifer Onion's dad is dropping her off so she can stay with you and Pinky while I'm gone."

"I hate Jennifer Onion," said Harris. "She's bossy."

"She can't boss you," said Grampa, "if you stay in bed."

Harris kept staring out the window.

"Come and look at this," he cried. "That crow is eating Pete's dogfood!"

Grampa leaned over and looked out the window.

"That dog has no backbone," he muttered.

They watched as the crow lined up another three pieces of kibble.

Harris glanced over at Grampa and thought his grandfather looked suddenly different. Younger, maybe. And he was smiling.

"That bird ..." said Grampa softly.

"Does it remind you of something?" blurted Harris. "Does it remind you of an old man? Or a baby? Or ..." he remembered what Mrs. Harder had said. "Or yourself?"

Grampa shook his head.

"Then what?" asked Harris.

"No," said Grampa. He shut his mouth tight and all the frown lines came back. "Into bed," he said abruptly. "It's late."

Harris was still awake when he thought he heard Jennifer Onion in the kitchen, talking to Grampa.

"You should keep the keys somewhere else," she said. "Then they won't fall off the hook into the garbage."

That was Jennifer Onion, all right. Bossy!

Harris heard Grampa go out, and then Jennifer Onion's music started playing from her laptop. It was all dumb music, about love gone wrong. *Looking for somebody like you ...* a voice sang, *just not you.* A long time later, Harris heard Grampa come back inside with Tessa.

"I'm never going to a dance again!" Tessa was saying. "The boys hid behind the gym mats, eating cookies, and the girls had to dance with each other all night."

She stomped upstairs to the bathroom. Then Harris heard her going past his room and into her own bedroom. Grampa paid the babysitter, and Harris heard the truck start so that Grampa could drive her home; and then, in a few minutes, he was back. After a while, Harris heard him going into his own room. A drawer opened, and Harris wondered if Grampa was eating the rest of the chocolate chips.

Because it was so late and Harris couldn't sleep, a restless feeling came over him. He padded around his room, looking at things—his floor-hockey stick and his football—but there wasn't really anything he wanted to do. He watched Chomper swim for a while. Then Harris drank all the water from his mug and used it to scoop up the fish along with a cup full of fish-water. Seen up close like this, Chomper was really beautiful, her rainbow-colored fins gleaming in the light of his bedside lamp.

The house was quiet. All Harris could hear was the water pump going on and off, on and off, and the furnace humming, and the wind outside, tugging at the side of the house. And in the stillness, he started wondering what the crow made Grampa think about. Something that made him happy for a moment, but then sad.

Harris thought about that. And then he thought about his teacher, and the sorrowfulness that she carried around. And Henry Harder. And Lucy. And Tessa. And then he thought about those lambs, stuck out there in that shed, far away from their mothers, if they even had mothers. And while he was thinking about all of those things, he wasn't thinking about being upside down in that slough, with the water coming in, and his father yelling, "Open that door, Harris. Open that door and get out!"

But as soon as Harris stopped thinking about all of those things, the water was waiting for him. As he forced his way out of the car, the water was right there. It rose up to meet him and he felt his shoes heavy with the cold weight of it. And the water kept on rising, over his head, burning his lungs and stealing his breath. And there was nothing he could do about it. Nothing he could do but let it happen.

CHAPTER ELEVEN

When Harris woke on Saturday morning, the house seemed strangely silent. He looked out his bedroom window into the dawn's first light and saw that the ground was covered in new snow, with more snow softly falling. Pete was inside his doghouse, staring mournfully at his empty food bowl. And Pete's water dish was covered with a film of ice.

"Winter's back!" groaned Harris. It was too early to get up, so he rolled himself into his Oilers quilt and went to sleep again, dreaming that he was a famous hockey player. And when he woke up for the second time, he could hear Grampa banging around in the kitchen, and Pinky yelling out "HUMPTY DUMPTY!" and dragging the big chairs around, and Tessa singing along to her iPod from the bedroom next door. It was definitely morning.

"Come on, kids," Grampa called. "Time to feed those lambs."

Harris threw on his clothes and ran down the stairs two at a time. Grampa had the bottles already made, and the four of them headed out through the slushy snow to the shed. Snow was still falling in big, fat flakes, and Pinky ran ahead to catch them on her tongue.

When they opened the door, Harris could see two of the lambs snuggled together under the heat lamp. They bleated when they saw their milk and charged toward Tessa and Pinky, latching onto the bottles and drinking greedily. The third lamb, though, the smallest one, was lying stiffly over in one corner.

"Oh, dear," said Grampa quietly, kneeling down and then throwing his jacket over the lamb. "I guess she didn't make it. Must have been something wrong with her to start with." He looked over at Harris. "It's just nature's way."

Harris stood there with the bottle of milk hanging down from one hand. He'd known there was something wrong with that lamb. He'd known it from the first, but his heart didn't want to listen. *Violet*. That was her name, and now she was gone. Slowly he walked back to the house and Grampa followed behind.

"That lamb just didn't have a chance, Harris," said Grampa gruffly as Harris dragged his feet up the back steps.

"I know it," said Harris.

"There must have been something wrong with her from the beginning, and that's why her mama wouldn't look after her," Grampa continued. "Sometimes that's just the way it is. It wasn't your fault. It wasn't your fault, Harris."

Those four words, those four simple words, opened something in Harris that he couldn't stop. It was as if a dam had broken and the river was raging out.

"IT WAS MY FAULT!" he yelled. Then he stormed into the house and up the stairs and into his room, where he started throwing things around. His lamp broke, and a picture fell off his wall, but he didn't care. He shoved open the window so the snow could just come in here, it could just come in here if it wanted! He didn't care. He didn't care about anything!

"Whoa, there, hold your horses," said Grampa, striding into the center of the storm and sitting down on Harris's bed. He reached out and grabbed Harris with his big hands and pulled him close. Harris felt his cheek pressed against Grampa's rough denim shirt.

"Now, let's just see here," said Grampa. "Let's just see here about this." He gently patted Harris on the back.

"I was in the water, but I could of ... I could of gone back," Harris said. "I could of gone back and got them out somehow. I just didn't. I ... I don't know why ... but I ... I just didn't!" He gave a dry sob, and then it all poured out, exactly as it had happened that day. Exactly as Harris had been thinking about it, or trying not to think about it, for all this time.

"Now hear this," said Grampa, when Harris had said all he had to say. "Now hear this, son. That wasn't your fault. That accident wasn't your fault at all, and there wasn't anything you could do. The RCMP and those paramedics even said as much. There wasn't anything you could do, and it was lucky, just lucky, that you made it out of there."

"No!" yelled Harris but Grampa's voice kept on.

"That was what they wanted, Harris," Grampa said evenly. "Their last moment on this earth was spent knowing you would be okay, and that gave them great happiness. It surely did." Now Grampa's voice had a big crack in it, but he kept on. "That's what you have to think of, son. That they knew," he said. "They knew you made it. And they were glad."

Harris felt the tears run down his cheeks. And he saw that Grampa was crying, too, while the snow blew through the window and landed everywhere. The snow blew in and fell over them both, and onto the furniture, and into the creases of the quilt on Harris's bed, dusting everything in white. Finally, Harris was all cried out and he heaved a deep sigh.

"Now then, how about some breakfast?" said Grampa, his voice husky.

"Okay," said Harris, wiping his face with the blanket. "Okay."

And just at that moment, a long black feather drifted down through the open window and onto the rug. A long black feather, coated with snow.

CHAPTER TWELVE

When Grampa pulled the truck into the Harders' farmyard later that Saturday morning, there were no animals in sight. But when Harris opened his door, all three dogs came running out of the barn. This time Harris was ready with the dog biscuits.

Tessa was home, babysitting Pinky, and Pete had stayed with them. After Harris filled his food bowl, Pete had gone back into his doghouse and refused to come out. Then Vinny had hopped in there with him. The last thing Harris saw when they left the yard was Pete curled up in his doghouse with Vinny crouched on his back.

"I don't blame you guys," Harris had told them. "As long as this snow is falling, I'd stay in there, too, if I were you!"

But the snow wasn't falling now. The sun was out and the snow was already melting. Big puddles lay all along the Harders' driveway.

Harris got out and patted the Harders' dogs and then gave them each a biscuit.

"Hey, Henry," called Grampa as Henry Harder came outside, pulling on his jacket. "How's Lucy today?"

"Not so good," said Henry. "She's forgotten herself again. So, really … not so good."

"Anything we can do?" asked Grampa.

"Thanks. No. Yesterday was a gift. A real gift, my friend," said Henry. He took the crate from Grampa, the crate they were using to bring Violet back, and set it out behind the barn. Then he went to get another orphan lamb from the pasture.

Harris took the crate with the new lamb to the back of the truck and pushed it inside. Another lamb. Here was another lamb, to take the place of Violet. Although nothing could really take the place of Violet. She had her own place, just as he remembered her.

Memory, thought Harris, *is an important thing.* He thought about this idea for a while, and then he thought: *When you lose someone, they're not completely gone.*

"But that's only part of it. That's not everything about memory," he whispered to himself. "Because it's complicated. It's way more complicated than that."

As they drove along, Grampa kept looking at his wrist. Finally, he said to Harris, "You haven't seen my watch, have you?"

Harris shook his head.

"I thought I'd left it on the dresser, but this morning it wasn't there."

Harris thought back to the last time he'd been in his grandfather's bedroom, getting those chocolate chips. He hadn't seen any watch. He was sure about that.

"I don't know," Harris said. "I haven't seen it."

When they got back home, Harris put the new lamb into the shed and Grampa made lunch. It was egg salad on buns, and Harris loved egg salad. He ate three of the buns while Pinky was tussling with Grampa about sitting in the highchair.

"You have to sit here, Ruth, or you can't have lunch," said Grampa.

"No," said Pinky. "No sit there!"

Finally, Grampa let her sit in a big chair if she sat on two phonebooks. And then she triumphantly held a whole bun in one hand and got egg all over her face.

After lunch, Tessa, Pinky, and Harris took out bottles of milk, and the new lamb sucked just as confidently as the other two.

That new lamb seemed to know just what the bottle was for. After the milk was done, though, the lambs kept bumping at their legs as if there was more milk around there somewhere. One of them even tried to suck on Pinky's elbow.

"They're pretty dumb," said Tessa.

"BALD DUMB!" crowed Pinky.

Then Harris remembered he hadn't fed his fish yet. He raced inside and tossed some fish food into the tank, but he couldn't see the guppy anywhere.

"Chomper?" he called, although he knew the fish couldn't hear him. "Chomper?"

He searched all around the tank, inside and out, but the fish wasn't there. Then his eye fell on the mug beside his bed. The mug where he'd caught Chomper last night to have a good look at him. But Chomper wasn't in the mug now. In fact, the mug was empty.

"Chomper!" yelled Harris. And then he yelled, "Tarnation!" And then in the next breath, he yelled, "PINKY!"

"What's wrong now? What's all the fuss about?" asked Grampa, coming into the room with Pinky at his heels.

"It's ... it's Chomper!" cried Harris. "PINKY DRANK CHOMPER!"

Pinky stood twisting her fingers into the front of the red T-shirt.

"Pinky," said Harris very slowly. "What—happened—to—my—fish?"

Pinky opened her mouth and pointed inside with her index finger.

"Uh," she said. "Uh-uh."

"Oh, no," moaned Harris. "She did it. She really did it. Bad girl. BAD GIRL, Pinky!"

Then three things happened. Pinky started to cry. Grampa charged out to phone the doctor to see whether Pinky was going to be okay. And Tessa pulled Pinky into her bedroom so that Harris could have some alone time.

Harris walked around his room a couple of times and thought about breaking things. The sound of Pinky's crying was loud in his ears, and he felt as if something inside him was swelling up until even his skin was stretched out. He looked at the fish tank and started to pick it up, but then he stopped himself. He didn't want to break that fish tank. It was Tessa's, and she'd probably make him pay for it.

He looked around at all his things. His lamp was cracked

from before and the picture frame had broken in half. Everything was all wrecked. Harris lay down on his quilt and buried his face in the pillow. He took a deep breath. He didn't think about Chomper. He didn't think about all the stuff he'd already broken. He thought surprisingly about Bana Manafort.

"Is okay?" she'd be asking in her quiet voice, if she was here right now. "Is okay?"

"Yeah," he muttered, even though he was sitting on his bed alone, and Bana Manafort wasn't anywhere near here. And suddenly he felt calmer.

Harris lay on his bed for a few more minutes and thought about hockey. His hockey season was done for now, but soon it would start up again. Fall wasn't that far away. And Harris was going to be a pro-hockey player. And he'd be famous. He thought about the Edmonton Oilers, his favorite team, and how they were going to be in the playoffs this year, after a streak of bad luck. They were going to be in the playoffs. And nothing could get them down. Not those Oilers. Then he let himself think about Chomper. He thought about Chomper until he was done thinking about him.

Finally, Harris knocked on Tessa's door. He could hear Pinky and Tessa talking, and when he opened the door, Tessa was sitting on the bed, showing Pinky her jewelry box. He sat down beside them and peered into the box. But it was empty. That box was empty.

"But where's all the treasure?" asked Harris.

"Well, it's just an empty old box," muttered Tessa, sounding a little embarrassed. "I used to keep some of Mom and Dad's stuff in here, to help me remember them. But then it seemed that I could remember them just as good when the box was empty. And then I sort of stopped wanting to think about them at all. Because every time I thought of them, I felt sad. So, I just kept the box locked up. And ... well ... then I kept Jason Beam's picture in here for a while." Tessa fiddled with the latch on the box.

"But last night I tore his picture up," she went on. "So now it's back to being my memory box again. And the stuff I remember about Mom and Dad ... it's still in here. It's all in here, just the way it was."

"Even though the box is empty?" Harris asked.

"Yeah. It's kind of weird. I can remember all sorts of stuff when the lid is open," said Tessa.

Harris looked at Pinky and he wanted to be cross with her still, because the anger had filled him up in a way that was kind of satisfying. But instead he leaned closer to his little sister. His sister, who hardly ever cried, but who had cried today. He could still see the stripes the tears had made on her chubby little cheeks.

"It ... it wasn't your fault," Harris said to Pinky. "It wasn't your fault. I shouldn't ... I shouldn't have left Chomper in that cup."

And saying those words somehow filled him up again, just as the anger had filled him up, but in a different way. In an even better way.

"But it wasn't really my fault, either," Harris went on. "It was ..." he stopped and sighed, and then he continued. "It was an accident."

"It was sushi," said Tessa.

"SUSHI," echoed Pinky.

"Sushi?" asked Harris.

"That's what they call raw fish when you eat it," Tessa explained. "Sushi."

"Yeah. Okay. It was sushi," said Harris. "Fine."

Pinky giggled.

"BALD SUSHI!" she said. And then Tessa and Harris giggled, too.

When Grampa came up to tell them that the doctor had said Pinky wouldn't die from eating the guppy, all three of them were still laughing like crazy.

"I don't know what happened to my key," Tessa said, when Grampa had gone back downstairs to make them some lunch. "I forgot to lock my treasure box last night, and when I woke up this morning, the key was gone."

"You really tore up Jason Beam's picture?" Harris asked, staring at his sister.

"He's a dork," said Tessa. "I think he wants to hang around with Molly Stringer after all."

"What ... what kinds of stuff can you remember about Mom and Dad?" asked Harris, eyeing the open box.

"Well ..." said Tessa. "I was telling Pinky about this time when I was five years old, and you were only two. I thought I was helping Mom bake a cake for these new neighbors, but instead I dumped a whole box of baking soda into it ..."

"I don't remember that," said Harris.

"And you fell off the piano bench and put your teeth through your bottom lip," Tessa said. "And while Mom and Dad were trying to decide whether to take you to the doctor, the neighbors showed up, and they sat in the living room by themselves eating that cake. And later, when we tasted the cake, it was horrible! It was really horrible! It had all that baking soda and Mom had forgotten the sugar. We found the sugar in a cup on the shelf. Anyways, when I took a bite, I actually spit it out, that cake was so awful. But those neighbors! Those poor neighbors! They each ate a huge piece!"

"I fell off a lot of things," said Harris.

"You were always jumping off things and getting hurt," Tessa said. "You've always had too much energy."

"I don't!" said Harris, but Tessa just nodded back.

"You do," she said.

Pinky reached over and pulled his little finger, and Harris burped.

"Disgusting!" said Tessa.

"No, you're disgusting!" Harris said.

"For the love of Pete, get along, you two!" called Grampa.

"We are getting along!" Harris yelled.

And then Pete started whining from the deck. He started whining in such a scaredy-cat way, and then he gave a yelp. Right away, Harris knew something was wrong. Something was really wrong.

Harris jumped down the stairs, two at a time, and then he ran to the back door to see what was the matter. And what he saw outside made him hold his breath. And what he saw after that was something really surprising.

CHAPTER THIRTEEN

Pete was pressed up against the glass door, whimpering, while four magpies ganged up in a circle of bullies. Every now and then, one of the birds would dart in and peck at him. And Pete wasn't doing anything to help himself.

Harris could see some nasty gashes under the dog's eyes, and there was a bloody scratch on his nose. Suddenly, like a dive bomber, a black shape torpedoed down on top of the magpies. Right, left, right, left, Vinny's wings flapped at them, while the crow's sharp beak pecked this way and that.

Before Harris could even open the door, three of the magpies had taken off. The fourth, a heavy-set bird that seemed almost too fat to fly, couldn't quite get itself into the air. Vinny watched it for a moment, and then looked over at Pete.

"*Caw*," said the crow. "*Caw-caw!*"

And then, as if in response, Pete bristled, stood up tall, and gave that old magpie one sharp nip on the tailfeathers. The magpie took a running leap off the step and flapped itself into the air and away.

"Vinny saved Pete!" yelled Harris, as both his sisters and Grampa came to see what all the fuss was about. "Vinny saved Pete and then Pete saved himself!"

"From what?" asked Tessa, peering outside.

"The magpies were bothering Pete again," Harris explained. "And Vinny chased most of them away! And Pete—scaredy-cat Pete—he chased the last one himself!"

As they all watched, Pete ran around the deck twice, barked sharply, and then pranced into his doghouse as if he was King of the Castle. In a minute, Vinny hopped in after him.

"Please, Grampa!" said Harris. "Please can we keep Vinny! That crow is part of our family! Vinny's part of our family, now!"

"Well, it looks like Pete's got himself a bodyguard," was all Grampa said.

"Or a coach," said Harris.

On Sunday morning, Harris watched Vinny dip three pieces of Pete's dry dogfood into his water dish and then eat them. And then three more.

"Vinny can count!" Harris cried, and Tessa came to the window to watch.

"Crows can't count," said Tessa.

"Just look!" cried Harris.

"I am looking," said Tessa. "And what I see is ... is ... MY NECKLACE!" she cried.

Harris looked at the doghouse and saw something shining from its dark interior. He watched as Tessa ran outside and, sure enough, she came back in with her necklace and a few other things. Grampa's gold watch. A little gold spoon. And a loonie.

"Look at what that thieving crow stole!" said Tessa.

"My watch!" said Grampa.

"My necklace and key," said Tessa.

"SPOON! MY SPOON!" said Pinky.

"My loonie!" said Harris. He didn't remember losing any money, but he'd gotten a loonie from Grenade, and who knew where it landed? When no one complained, he tucked the loonie into his pocket.

Finders keepers, he thought.

And then he thought about that crow. It remembered so many things: how to get into their house, where to keep its shiny things, and how to count to three. It seemed to remember everything. And suddenly Harris knew what he should add to his science fair poster. If he were going to prove that crows had good memories, he needed to list all those examples from Vinny.

CHAPTER FOURTEEN

On Monday morning, Harris put his finished poster on Mrs. Featherbuster's desk.

"I knew you could do it," she told him. Something about her looked different. She looked different somehow.

"I knew I could, too!" said Harris. He looked at his teacher's face. Something had changed but he couldn't quite name it.

The school day began, as usual, with Bell Work. They had to write down as many ideas as they could under the heading *Gemstones and Precious Minerals*. When Mrs. Featherbuster had collected their notebooks, she asked them to come and sit in the story corner.

When Harris sat down, he saw that Mrs. Featherbuster had placed a white cloth on the carpet, and in the middle of it sat a big lump of golden yellow.

"Gold!" the kids around him whispered. "Is that real gold?"

"Yes, that's a lump of gold," said their teacher. "And as we all know, gold is a precious mineral that can be found in the earth, and it is worth a lot of money." She looked at them and cleared her throat.

"Someone gave that lump of gold to me when I was just a child, and I'd forgotten all about it," she went on. "I'd forgotten all about it until just last week. Mr. Vinny, an old man in my neighborhood, gave a gold nugget to each of us kids. Just before he left. And he said to keep it for when we needed it the most."

The teacher smiled at them all.

"How did he get them, those gold nuggets?" asked Marsha Abbot.

"He went sluicing for gold. In the Klondike, I think," said Mrs. Featherbuster. "During the gold rush, people built wooden troughs called sluice boxes, and put them into creeks and rivers. Then they shoveled gravel into them, and the running water separated out the sand and stones from any larger pieces of gold."

"Wow, that would be so cool," breathed Mike Morin.

"Well, when I was young," the teacher went on, "I didn't need to sell this gold. I had everything I wanted. And then when I had some tough times, I'd think about the gold. And I'd think of what

I could do if I sold it. And then I'd decide to just save it a little longer, for when I needed it more."

She smiled at them again.

"And when I found it this weekend, where I'd packed it away, my first thought was to sell it and quit my job and travel the world!"

There was a murmur from the students. Surely not—Mrs. Featherbuster couldn't be leaving them!

"But I decided once again to save it for later. When I need it more. Because I really like my job. I like all of you. And who knows if I'd be happier traveling the world than being right here!"

The children broke into applause.

"We're glad!" said Jessica Shewchuk. "It would be awful to have a new teacher!"

"You. You're one best!" said Bana Manafort.

"You rock," said Mike Morin.

"Well, you're a good class and I'm having fun here," said Mrs. Featherbuster. "And I want you all to know that I am proud of your science projects. I think we could win the Grade 4 Living Science Award today. But if we don't, that's okay, too. We've done good work and you should all be proud of that."

While they had Silent Reading, Mrs. Featherbuster made

her own poster about the lump of gold. Harris saw the title. *My Crowning Glory*, she'd written, and she listed off all sorts of different things she could do with that gold, if she wanted. He couldn't quite see the last thing on the list, but the word *hope* was in it. He saw the word *hope*, and then Mrs. Featherbuster picked up a book to remind him that it was reading time. And so he had to go back to the library corner.

Mrs. Featherbuster took one last look at their work to make sure everything was spelled right, and then she sent the whole class down to the front hallway with lots of tape.

"Make sure you hang everything up straight," she said, "where the judges can get a good look at it. I'll come and hang mine up at the end—maybe we'll get extra points for teacher participation!"

The rest of the morning flew by. They had math, and recess, and then gym. And Mrs. Featherbuster let them play that Cree game again: *Pitisowewepahikan*.

After lunch, Harris stood proudly beside his poster. He'd put it as close to the big front doors as possible, thinking his work would really stand out there. Suddenly, he looked through the glass and there was Vinny, tap-tapping to get in. Harris quickly opened one of the doors and that crow flew right into the school, as if it belonged there. It circled around the hallway, and then it came back to rest on the table beside Harris's poster.

Its feathers still looked bedraggled. And the fluff on the top of its head still seemed down on its luck. But Vinny's eyes were bright and shiny, if just a little bit sad, and the crow's wrinkled feet danced around on that table as if it were doing a jig.

"Look!" said a couple of kids, and then a couple more. "Look! A crow's in the school!"

Just at that very moment, one of the interns in the kindergarten class came walking by and, as soon as Vinny saw her, that crow started flapping and cawing and then singing out a series of long, clear notes.

"Kibble?" said the intern, rushing over. "Kibble, is that you!" A diamond stud in one of her nostrils caught the light and sparkled as the crow sang another series of notes. Then it jumped onto her shoulder.

"Well, this is an amazing surprise!" said the intern. "Where did you find him?"

"I ... well ..." Harris started.

"My kids will be so happy!" said the intern, reaching up to pat the crow. "They've missed you so much, you wise old bird."

"Your … your kids?" asked Harris.

"I have three. The oldest is Emily. She's in Grade 8. And then there's Owen, and he's about your age. In fact, he looks a little bit like you. And then there's Petra, and she's only two. She cried for days after we lost him. And, of course, there's our dog, Buddy. Kibble used to ride around on his back." She reached up again to pat the crow.

"It's so good we found him!" she said.

"*Caw,*" said the crow, and Harris thought he saw the bird's feathers straighten just a little bit and its expression lift. "*Caw-caw!*"

"How did … how did Vinny get lost? I mean Kibble," asked Harris, and his mouth was dry.

"I brought him to school for Show and Tell, earlier this month," said the intern. "Then he must have followed me to school again and gotten lost. How did he find you?"

"Well," said Harris. "It all started like this." And he told how Vinny had pecked at his bedroom window, and about Pinky calling it a bluebird, and about how it taught Pete to fight, and how it watched him and Tessa through the bus window.

"Your family is the same as ours," the intern said. "Three kids and a dog!"

"Like I said on my poster," he told her. "Crows can count."

The intern looked at his work and nodded her head.

"You've done a spectacular job here," she said. "I like it where you have all those examples of Kibble's good memory."

"I know," said Harris. "I just added that part this morning."

She finished reading the poster and then turned and looked at him. "I'm sorry to take him away from you," she said. "I can tell you care about him, too."

"I guess your kids have been really sad," mumbled Harris. "And he was yours first."

"Thanks for understanding," she said. "I really appreciate it. Maybe sometime you can come to visit."

"That's okay," said Harris. "That's ... it's okay. But ... but could I keep Vinny ... Kibble ... for the science fair? Maybe you could come back here at last recess? That's when we'll be cleaning up."

"Well, of course!" said the intern. "That would work great! Boy, will my kids ever be happy tonight." The intern gave the crow a little nudge, and it jumped back onto the table.

"Stay," she said, looking at it. Then she looked at Harris. "See you later."

"See you," said Harris.

"*Caw. Caw-caw,*" said the crow.

Harris tried to smile as she turned and walked away down the hall, but his lips kind of trembled a bit, and he thought about how *Kibble* was a dumb name for a crow.

"A crow!" said a bunch of kids who had gathered around his table. "A real crow!"

"Come back in a minute," said Harris, pulling down his poster. "We're not quite ready."

He couldn't prove that all crows had a good memory. That wasn't very scientific, when the only experience he had was with one crow. But he could tell the story of his crow. At least ... it was his crow for now.

When Harris set the poster on the table beside Vinny, the crow hopped and flapped and looked down at the paper, as if to say, "Well, what are you waiting for!"

First, Harris turned the poster over. Next, he went and got a black marker from the office and began writing all sorts of things on the fresh side of the paper. He wrote about the day the crow came into his life, and all the talents it had, such as being able to count, and finding a new family a lot like its real family, and then how its real family found it at last. And then he put the title in extra big letters at the top: *The Case of the Missing Crow: Narrative Non-Fiction*. The subtitle, underneath, was *What a Crow Has Taught Me About Memory*. And underneath that, he printed in capital letters, "BY HARRIS ALBERT OLSON."

"*Do all crows have good memories?*" he wrote at the bottom of the poster. "*Or just this one? Maybe these are questions we can't answer now, but hopefully someday we'll know more about bird brains and how they compare to human brains.*"

"Memories," he wrote in a sidebar along one side, "are like a bunch of rocks and minerals that you find when you're sluicing for gold. Some memories you want to keep, because they help you out. And bring you joy. Or hope. Those ones are the gold. And some memories you just have to let go of. You have to let go of them if you can. Because they're just sand and gravel."

When he taped the poster back up on the wall, all the kids pushed closer to read it and look at the crow.

"Is that your crow?" kids kept asking. "Is that the crow that can count?"

"No and yes," Harris told them.

Bana Manafort stepped away from her poster to look more closely at Vinny, and she smiled.

"Is beautiful!" she breathed. "Not beautiful like my crows, my gray and black crows, but beautiful. Canadian!" Her hand slipped into his, for just a moment, and Harris was surprised at how small and warm it was. And how strong it felt, gripping his own.

"Is okay?" she asked Harris.

"Yeah," he said. "Yeah. Thanks."

When the judges finally came by, Harris was getting tired of talking, but he answered their questions as best he could. And they had a lot of them.

"How old can a crow get?" one judge asked.

"The oldest known American crow was 29½ years old," Harris said.

"Do crows leave Saskatchewan in the winter?" asked another of the judges.

"Yes, they fly out of Canada to the lower plains in the United States: Nebraska, Kansas, and Oklahoma. And then they come back to Canada in the spring," said Harris.

More questions followed, and Harris answered them in a kind of blur.

"In addition to knowing about your crow, I see that you have a lot of additional knowledge about crows in general," said the last of the judges. She was an older woman with big black glasses that made her eyes look like marbles. "What sources did you use to prepare for this project?"

"Well, I used the Internet and the school library," Harris said, showing her the three books he'd borrowed to do his research. "And I talked to the librarian, and kids in my class, and my best friend, and my sisters, and my grandfather. And my neighbors. I talked to everyone about crows, and that is how I learned all this stuff."

"Very good," said the judge. "Using multiple sources, that's impressive! And you have used original source material, too. First-hand observations of a real crow! Good work!"

"Thanks," said Harris.

"I'm an ornithologist," said the judge. "Do you know what that is?"

"No," said Harris. "Maybe. Is it an eye doctor?"

"That's *ophtha*-mologist," said the judge. "I'm an *ornith*-ologist. A scientist who studies birds."

"Oh," said Harris. "Wow." He hadn't known that you could do that. Be a scientist that only studied birds.

"Do you know ... what is the best part of your project?" asked the judge.

"Well ..." started Harris, looking first at Vinny and then at his work.

"It's the questions you are asking to guide further research," she told him, straightening her glasses and staring at the bottom of his poster. "The very best studies leave us wanting more information, and direct us how to find it."

"Oh," said Harris. "Oh. Good."

When Tessa's class came by to look at the posters, his sister made a beeline for Harris.

"That's not the same poster you made at home!" she said.

"No," said Harris. "I revised it."

She stood and read what he'd written.

"So, you have to give the crow back?" she asked, when she'd finished.

"Its real family misses it," he said. "But ..." he sighed, "... maybe I can go and visit."

"This is good," she said, rereading some of the words on the poster. "It's kind of like a story. But it's all true."

"That's what narrative non-fiction is," said Harris.

Then Tessa reread the sidebar out loud. *Some memories ... help you out ... And some ... you just have to let go of ... if you can.*"

She nodded and looked at him and her eyes were kind of shiny.

"That's right," she said. "That's exactly right."

"Thanks," said Harris.

"It's hard to do, though," said Tessa softly. "It's hard to let go of those ones."

"Yes," said Harris. "But there's ways. I know there's ways."

Tessa kept staring at his poster.

"I had a fight with Mom that night you all left for the hockey game," she blurted. "I wanted to sleep over at a friend's and Mom said, 'No.' She said I had to help Grampa with Ruth because she was teething. And when Dad came to tell me goodbye, I wouldn't open my bedroom door. I was mad at both of them. And that's the last time ..." she gulped, and her voice, when she spoke again, was just a whisper. "That's the last time ... well, you know." Her cheeks were wet.

"But think of all the times you didn't fight with 'em," said Harris after a minute. "You gotta think about that."

"I know," said Tessa. "I guess I know that." She rubbed a sleeve across her face. Then she looked at his poster again.

"I think you're going to be a storyteller when you grow up," she told him. "Just like Grampa. Just like Grampa used to be, I mean."

"Nah," said Harris.

"I think your poster's the best!" she added.

"That's because you haven't looked at any of the other posters," grinned Harris. "But thanks, anyways."

Tessa started to walk away. Then she darted back. "Remember that Grampa's picking us up after school. So don't get on the bus! You always forget stuff like that!"

"I don't!" said Harris. "I wasn't going to."

"*Caw*," said the crow. "*Caw-caw!*"

And this time it sounded as if that old crow was laughing.

Harris saw Henry Harder and his wife Lucy making their way through the crowd. Henry had Lucy by the elbow, and he was steering her over to them as best he could.

"There," said Henry Harder, when they got close. "There's that crow, Lucy. You saw it with Harris the other day."

The crow flapped its wings and preened a little bit.

"That crow," said Lucy, "is a—a rascal." She looked at Harris and smiled. "What about a doughnut?"

"Okay," said Harris and smiled back. "Absolutely!"

Henry Harder winked at Harris and his face kind of glowed. It wasn't exactly joy but something else. Harris looked carefully at Henry Harder. *Hope.* It was *hope* he saw there, written on Henry Harder's face as if it had been spelled right out.

Then Henry Harder read through the poster, every word. And he said, "I like your work, Harris. Especially that one part. The part about memory. You've got it right. You've sure got it right, son."

"*Caw,*" said the crow again. "*Caw-caw!*"

Finally, just as the students were starting to put everything away, Grampa appeared, lugging Pinky on his hip.

"Well, well," he said, breathing heavily and striding over to Harris. "This looks very fine indeed. *The Case of the Missing Crow!* Maybe you're going to be a detective. Or a lawyer! Maybe you'll be a lawyer, after all, just like me!"

"I'm going to be a pro-hockey player," said Harris. "Or a bird scientist. Or maybe," he added, "a storyteller ... but probably not all that. Probably just a hockey player."

Pinky squirmed out of Grampa's arms and hugged Harris around the knees. He patted her on the head, where her hair was starting to grow back, and then watched as Grampa's eyes passed over the poster. When Grampa got to the sidebar, he tilted his head and leaned in to read more carefully. Then a shadow seemed to cross his face and he turned away, grabbing Pinky by the hand.

"I'm taking her to the playground," he said gruffly. "And then we'll be in the parking lot to drive you home. Just come out when you're ready."

CHAPTER FIFTEEN

After the Grade 4 students had moved their posters back to the classroom, they waited with their teacher for the results of the Science Fair. When the news came in, Mrs. Featherbuster called them together in the story corner. She called them all together, and she read them the email thanking them for their participation. And she told them she was proud of them.

"I'm supremely proud of all of you," she said. "This was the best science fair ever!"

"But who won?" asked Marsha Abbott. "Who won?"

"Well, our class did not win," said Mrs. Featherbuster. "But Dundurn didn't win, either," she added, and Harris thought he saw a glint in her eye that was kind of like gold. A glint that was kind of like gold and kind of like *vindication*.

"Dundurn didn't win," she said again. "It was another town. Colonsay. Colonsay won. They've got this new teacher there who put all the posters on some sort of online wiki so families could read them at home. So probably Colonsay deserved to win."

Mrs. Featherbuster smiled at her students.

"But I know your posters were the best," she said. "For sure, they were absolutely the very best, in my estimation, and you should all be very, very proud. And one other thing. Someone among us has won a new prize this year. It's a prize for Most Original Project. Let's all cheer for Harris Olson!"

Harris looked at his teacher in surprise. Then he looked over at Jessica Shewchuk, but she was staring down at her desk. Bana Manafort caught his eye though. She caught his eye and grinned.

"Well, I'll be," he said. "Tarnation."

"Your certificate will come in the mail," Mrs. Featherbuster said. "And when it does, please bring it to school. I'm sure we'd all like to see it."

"Okay," said Harris. "Yeah, okay."

Everybody clapped, and Harris looked around at his class-mates, a bit surprised to hear them clapping. They were clapping for him. And what Harris was thinking, what he was thinking at that very moment was this: *I'm still going to be a pro-hockey*

*player. But maybe I'll also be a detective or a lawyer. Or maybe
a scientist. I could be a scientist and study stuff. Not everything.
Just birds. Or maybe just crows.*

When Harris walked out to the school bus, he felt a little lonely
knowing that Vinny was gone. But his spirits lifted as Grenade
ran over and yelled, "Can you come to my place after supper?
There's no Track tonight and we could play floor hockey!"

"I'll ask," said Harris. "Or you could come to my house! You
could help feed the lambs!"

"I'll ask!" said Grenade. "I bet Mom will drive me over later.
And I can bring a cake. She made two of 'em yesterday and they're
not very good, so she'll probably want to get rid of one!"

"Lambs," said Jessica Shewchuk. She was standing right
behind Harris. "Lambs! Oh, cute!" He turned around and
looked straight into her big green eyes. And they looked greener
than ever.

"They're not all that cute," Harris blurted. "If you really want
to know, these lambs are mostly so stupid that their cuteness gets
sucked out by dumbness."

"Oh, well, I think they're cute," she said. "I have a toy lamb
that I used to sleep with when I was a little kid."

"Oh," Harris said and looked down at his feet.

"I call it Lambie McLamb Face," she said.

"Oh," he said again. He thought about the lambs and how smelly they were. And how they had to be carried everywhere. Who'd want to sleep with them? Nobody! Then he looked back at Jessica Shewchuk. Everything about her kind of shone. Even her nose shone. She had the shiniest nose Harris had ever seen.

"Well, bye," she said.

"Bye," said Harris, and walked over to Grampa's truck. When he got inside, he saw that Pinky was asleep in her car seat and Grampa was fiddling with the radio. Suddenly, a song came on that Harris knew.

"Hey, that's Gramma's song!" cried Harris. And then he wished he hadn't said it. Grampa quickly set the radio to a different station. And all that was playing there was the weather.

"Why can't we ever talk about her," muttered Harris. "We can't ever talk about her."

"Well," Grampa started. "I don't need to talk about—"

"I want to talk about her!" said Harris. "I want to know why it happened and WHY WE CAN'T TALK ABOUT HER!"

"Hush now, Harris," said Grampa. "I don't have to—"

"Tell it," said Harris. "You just tell it!" His face felt hot, as if he were going to explode.

"Well, Harris. Calm down. Calm down, now. It's not really a secret," Grampa began quietly. "It ... it's just that it's hard for me." Grampa stopped talking and Harris could see, in Grampa's face, that he was having some kind of argument with himself. And that a decision was being made. When Grampa started to speak again, his voice was slow but steady.

"Well, it was a Saturday morning," Grampa said. "And ... and I was going out to work. And I thought I'd put out my cigarette before I left, but I guess I hadn't. And the wind came up and blew some papers over my desk. And Gramma was still sleeping. So, when ... when the fire started. Everything burned so fast. And there wasn't any way ... and she was gone. And everything was just gone."

The two of them sat still for a moment in the front of the truck.

"But it was an accident," Harris whispered. "That was an accident, Grampa."

"No," said his grandfather steadily. "No, I guess it was just my own fool stupidity to forget to put out that cigarette."

"It was an accident," Harris repeated.

"Well, maybe. Maybe it was," said Grampa in a small, tight voice. "But that doesn't bring her back. It won't bring her back."

"I don't remember anything about her, really," said Harris. "Except the popcorn. And the lemonade. And the singing."

Grampa didn't say anything for a moment. When he finally spoke, his voice broke a few times.

"Well, there was a lot more to her than that, son," he said. "There surely was a lot more to all of them than I guess we talk about."

"I don't remember much about ... about anyone ..." said Harris. And Grampa coughed and pulled out a Kleenex to blow his nose. And then they just sat quietly and listened to the rest of the weather report. When Tessa banged on the side of the truck, Grampa unlocked the back door.

"Jason Beam's invited me to go over there for Sunday supper," she cried as she launched herself into the truck. "Can I, Grampa? Go there for Sunday supper?"

"Sunday supper?" Grampa asked. He bit his lip. "Tarnation. Are his parents going to be there?"

"Of course!" said Tessa. "They're cooking it, aren't they? And they've invited me to go."

"Well. Maybe," said Grampa. He heaved a deep sigh. "Maybe.

Let me think about it. You're a new generation, you kids. Sometimes I forget that." They watched as the last of the school buses left the parking lot, and then Grampa started the truck. As he put the truck in reverse and pulled his foot off the brake, he took another big breath. "Okay," he said, finally. "All right, Tessa. You can go. You can go to Jason Beam's for Sunday supper. But you'll have to come home right afterwards and help with the lambs."

"And can I get a tattoo?" asked Tessa. "A bunch of kids in my class have one."

"What? No!" said Grampa. "One thing at a time, okay? Sunday supper is good enough for now."

"Rats!" said Tessa. Then she pulled out her phone. "I'm texting Jason Beam this minute."

"Spare me the details," said Grampa.

"Has Vinny gone?" Tessa asked suddenly. "Harris, has Vinny already gone to that other family?"

"Yeah," said Harris.

"I miss that crow already," said Tessa. And then she started texting.

"Can Grenade come over tonight for a sleepover?" asked Harris.

"A sleepover? Well, maybe. I suppose he could," said Grampa. "We've got some extra quilts in the cupboard that ... that your Gramma made. You know she made all those quilts for you kids," he said, his voice heaving a bit. "She sewed them with her own hands and a lot of love. Anyways, there's all those extra ones she made in there. Grenade can use a couple of those."

"His mom's sending a cake!" Harris said. "Grenade said it won't taste very good, but it's probably not as bad as that cake Tessa made once where she forgot the sugar." He grinned at Tessa, remembering her story of the failed cake.

"It's *Renae*," corrected Tessa. "Why do we always call him *Grenade* when it's really *Renae*."

"Have I ever told you," said Grampa, "about the time I made a cake that was hard as a rock? It was for your Mom's birthday, and I guess something was wrong with the recipe. I got it off the Internet."

"You can't just download *anything* off the Internet, Grampa," scolded Tessa. "What site did you use?"

"Tell about the cake!" interrupted Harris.

"I don't remember the site," said Grampa. "But the cake was gingerbread, and I lost a filling from one of my front teeth when I bit into it."

Harris and Tessa giggled.

"Easy for you to laugh!" said Grampa. "But I'm a better cook now, wouldn't you say?"

"Yes!" said Harris. "Especially Al's Famous Steak!"

"Well, you're in luck," chuckled Grampa. "That's what we're having for supper."

"Do we have any fruit punch?" asked Harris suddenly.

Grampa nodded.

"And ginger ale?"

"I think so," Grampa said.

"Because I'm going to make us Ambrosia," cried Harris. "We can have that for supper, too!"

When they got home, there were lambs to feed and then it was suppertime, and then, before Grenade came over, Harris went to work on that picture. That picture of everyone. He took it out from behind his desk and laid it out flat. Then he got his pencil crayons and started drawing.

First, he drew Grampa standing beside the three of them, right beside him and Tessa and Pinky. Grampa's hair stuck up all over, just like his own hair. And Grampa's arms looked kind of empty, so Harris drew the fiddle in there, as if Grampa was getting ready to play something. Then he added Henry Harder, and Lucy, and Mrs. Featherbuster, and the gold nugget. And then he added Vinny, over in one corner. And a pile of colorful quilts, all sewed up with Gramma's love.

Harris thought for a minute, and then he got a couple of pastel crayons and sketched Violet, way up at the top. And then, beside Violet, he added Mom. And Dad. And Gramma. They were all looking down like angels. And he used his thumb to smudge them, just a bit, so they were kind of blurry. Like those water lilies in Grampa's poster.

Dad had red hair. Just like he did. And Mom had freckles on her face. Just like his freckles. And Gramma had a great big smile. Just like his smile. He thought he'd forgotten them. But he hadn't, not really. Once he started to draw, he realized they'd been here all along. All of them had been here all along.

Mom and Dad are angels, he thought, *and they are marching around up there with the Saints. And Violet. And Gramma. And they are all watching over.*

He thought suddenly about Chomper, and so he added him, too, but in a bowl on the ground, not up in God's heaven. He somehow didn't think a fish belonged in the air.

As Harris looked at the picture, something in him lifted as if he owned that gold nugget himself. There was still room to draw other stuff if he wanted. Lots of room. And later, he'd write about all of it. He'd write it down in one of his old school notebooks. All that he could remember, so that when Pinky grew up, she'd remember, too. All about the Ambrosia and how he got his name from Grampa. And about the diamond ring commercial, and how Mom said she didn't want a bigger rock. And Pinky yelling Humpty Dumpty and making him and Grampa laugh. And cutting off all her hair. And Grampa's Super Deluxe Eggs and Al's Famous Steaks. And Tessa's cake. And how he fell and put his two teeth through his bottom lip.

He pondered for a moment.

And Gramma's quilts, and her lemonade and popcorn. And the singing.

He thought some more.

He thought about the story of how Pete learned to be brave. And the story of how Pinky drank Chomper. And the story of Violet. And how warm and strong Bana Manafort's hand had felt in his own. And all about Vinny. And all about everything.

"And I won't lock it up," he said out loud. "Not like that old jewelry box. I'll keep my notebook open all the time. Pinky can look inside whenever she wants. And anyone can. Anyone else who might want to read this stuff."

And as he spoke, he thought he saw something outside his window.

A flicker of wings.

A shiny black eye.

But when he looked again, that crow was gone.

At least, it was gone for now ...

ACKNOWLEDGMENTS

A special thank you to Deb Amundson, a caring and observant teacher who shared with me the truly amazing story of a real counting pet crow that came to school.

Gratitude, as always, to Peter Carver—my ever-patient editor and friend to all readers, young and old—as well as the team at Red Deer Press for their spectacular support.

Thanks also to the Saskatoon Public Schools' Brightwater Site for instructions on *Pitisowewepahikan* / Double Ball, and Brenda Kalyn for her inspirational gym classes, and Anna Johnson for sharing her gift of music. Song lyrics included in this novel are credited as follows: "When the Saints Go Marching In" is an African-American Spiritual famously recorded in 1938 by Louis Armstrong; Gramma's song "Yellow Submarine" was written by the Beatles; "Swing Low, Sweet Chariot" is an African-American Spiritual attributed to Wallis Willis around 1865.

Thank you to colleagues Geraldine and Tim for their information about sluicing gold. And huge appreciation to the University of Saskatchewan for the sabbatical during which this story was first conceived, as well as the Hambidge Center, Georgia, for the time and space to develop my work in a community with our group leader Christine and my other fellow artists: Leela, Iddo, Rebecca, Perry, Amy, Ame, Phyllis, Rose, Wyatt, Kristin, Ryder, Donna, Anna, Kim, and, of course, my wonderful husband Dwayne.

INTERVIEW WITH BEV BRENNA

What made you want to tell this story?

About fifteen years ago, a teacher friend told me a true story about a real crow that started hanging around a school playground. The crow finally moved in with a nearby family who soon discovered the crow's original owners. And, amazingly, both families had three little girls with long blonde hair (and a dog). The idea of a counting crow with a good memory inspired me to try to tell this story in a variety of ways. After a few failed attempts, including a picture-book draft that didn't work out, I began my journey into this novel about Harris, who is dealing with the death of his parents.

What led you to using the crow as a character?

As Harris trudges into the difficult parts of his story, he needs a character to guide him safely through. I'm always reluctant to have adults solve the problems of children, because I think that kids are pretty capable of figuring things out, sometimes with a little help. When I wrote the first chapter of this book, with the crow landing on Harris's bedroom floor with a solid kind of thud, I knew right away that this crow would be more than just a distraction from Harris's problems. Very soon, the crow in this story became a mentor for Harris, helping him deal with his memories.

How do you, as a writer, go about choosing the names for the characters in your story?

I encountered the name "Harris" years ago as the name of a friend's youngest son, and it kind of stuck with me as the name of an acreage boy I would someday write about. I'm usually unaware of naming any characters "after" anyone, and none of my characterizations are real people, but the boy I created in my mind as Harris became so clear to me that I hoped he would be a strong protagonist for this book.

The name "Featherbuster" catapulted onto the page as soon as I started writing about Harris's teacher, and once I'd begun to see her in the story as Mrs. Featherbuster, there was no turning back. Even though her character has some serious things to say, I think her name, and Harris's response to it, lighten the mood of the story at times. With her bright floral dress and her generous smile, I think she really is larger than life, just as her name suggests.

The three Olson children look after baby lambs who are orphans and need to be fed to survive. Why did you include this in your story?

My husband and I spent eighteen years on an acreage in rural Saskatchewan, raising our three sons. Some of the experiences we had on that acreage found their way into this book as experiences Harris and his siblings have. We did collect orphan lambs and care for them, and they provided terrific learning experiences for us all. One of the benefits of farm life is the chance to observe life cycles in nature that are part of the bigger scheme of things. I think Harris's experience with Violet helps him talk about the loss of his parents in ways he wasn't previously able to do.

Other stories in the book stem from real life experiences, as well. One of my sons actually did drink his brother's fish from a cup of water on a bedside table, and similar pandemonium occurred.

A number of people are sad, for different reasons, in this story: young people as well as adults. But, in the end, they overcome that sadness. So it is not an unhappy story after all. Why was that important to you?

I think kids need to know that sadness is part of the human experience. Through the complicated lives of characters we read about, we can all learn vicariously about resilience and hope. For me, presenting opportunities to overcome challenges is a key part of writing. Not that every story should have a happy ending, but I think that throughout life, we build positive strategies to learn and grow, and I want my stories to show that growth. Seeing positive outcomes is also why I enjoy reading books written for young people. I think books for this audience shine with positivity about the future, and I appreciate that optimism.

Why do you think it's possible for people to get rid of the sadness in their lives—as Harris and others do here?

I don't know anyone who has been sad their whole life. Even people in the most difficult situations often find ways to experience joy. I also don't know anyone who has been happy their whole life. Sadness and joy are both part of the human experience. How we endure the difficulties and find ways to go on are key to understanding what it is to be human. I think that reading about how characters manage their challenges gives us all new ideas for coping and support.

"There are some themes, some subjects, too large for adult fiction; they can only be dealt with adequately in a children's book." These words were spoken by celebrated author Philip Pullman when he received a big award in the United Kingdom some years ago. Would you agree with what he says? Why?

This is an interesting quote, because there was a time when children's literature stayed away from lots of themes and subjects we see in kids' books now. Contemporary kids have access to much more information these days, especially through digital connections. Because of this, I think it becomes the job of children's literature to help young readers process uneasy subject matter.

In *Because of That Crow*, a child experiences the traumatic aftermath of a terrible accident. The somewhat magical circumstances that unfold help him to come to terms with his parents' death and forge ahead with his life. Perhaps this would never happen in real life. But ... I think it could! I'd rather live with this kind of hope than the alternative. And I'd rather children lived with this kind of hope as well. How will we ever solve the world's problems, or our own, if we don't believe that we can?

Notice how I've veered away from actually answering the question here about what adult fiction can do. I have to confess that I don't really read a lot of adult fiction. I much prefer children's books!

What would you say to young writers who want to include in their stories unhappy moments or events, but may have been warned off that approach by teachers or parents?

I think writing can be a healthy way to deal with our own unhappy moments or events. But I also think that overly dwelling on sad times through our writing can make us miserable. If what we are writing is bringing us peace or satisfaction, then I suggest we use that as a measure of whether or not we should continue. Some of the sections in *Because of That Crow* were difficult for me to write because I was drawing on my own experiences of the loss of loved ones. But in the end, I'm happy that I was able to work through my own feelings of grief and loss in the safe context of a story.

Thank you, Bev, for your thoughtful insights.